About the

Zelda Rhiando was born in Dublin in 1973 and read English Literature at Cambridge. She lives in South London with her husband, two
daughters and four cats. Fukushima Dreams is her second novel.

FUKUSHIMA DREAMS

FUKUSHIMA DREAMS

ZELDA RHIANDO

This edition first published in 2018

Unbound

6th Floor Mutual House, 70 Conduit Street, London W1S 2GF

www.unbound.com

ISBN (eBook): 978-1-11586-89-0

ISBN (Paperback): 978-1-911586-88-3

Design by Mecob

Printed in Great Britain by Clays Ltd, St Ives Plc

MIX
Paper from
responsible sources
FSC® C018072

For Kitty, who ignited the writing flame, and then kept it alight

Dear Reader,

The book you are holding came about in a rather different way to most others. It was funded directly by readers through a new website: Unbound.

Unbound is the creation of three writers. We started the company because we believed there had to be a better deal for both writers and readers. On the Unbound website, authors share the ideas for the books they want to write directly with readers. If enough of you support the book by pledging for it in advance, we produce a beautifully bound special subscribers' edition and distribute a regular edition and e-book wherever books are sold, in shops and online.

This new way of publishing is actually a very old idea (Samuel Johnson funded his dictionary this way). We're just using the internet to build each writer a network of patrons. Here, at the back of this book, you'll find the names of all the people who made it happen.

Publishing in this way means readers are no longer just passive consumers of the books they buy, and authors are free to write the books they really want. They get a much fairer return too – half the profits their books generate, rather than a tiny percentage of the cover price.

If you're not yet a subscriber, we hope that you'll want to join our publishing revolution and have your name listed in one of our books in the future. To get you started, here is a £5 discount on your first pledge. Just visit unbound.com, make your pledge and type TASHI18 in the promo code box when you check out.

Thank you for your support,

Dan, Justin and John
Founders, Unbound

Super Patrons

Kate Hamilton
Finbar Hawkins
Kevin Hinde
Paul Holmes
Koreen Hubbard
Cait Hurley
Tessa Kellett
Jacky Kenna
Alexandria Kenna
Farouk Laifa
Steve Langkamp
Deborah Liddlow
Chris Locke
Tom Loosemore
Juan Lopez-Valcarcel
Simon Lucy
Stefan Magdalinski
Rod McLaren
Fiona Middleton
Desiree Miloshevic
Jennifer Moate
Edward O'Rourke
Louise Oldfield
Scott Pack
Caroline Paterria
Neil Pepper
Jessica Pigg
Alex Pilcher
Elizabeth Piper
Paul Pod
Czarmé, Kevin, Abigael & Donovan Pooley
Gareth Pym
Billy Rizcallah
Jude Robinson
Kass Schmitt
Christian Shields

Shula Sinclair
Ross Sleight
Konrad Slusarski
Keith Smith
Michelle Swallow
Steven Taylor
Boz Temple-Morris
Tom Tomaszewski
Mark Turner
Jo Twist
Sharon Tynan
Sheila Urbanoski
Tom Watson
Meg Watson
Sophia Yates

With grateful thanks to Alexandria Kenna who helped make this book happen.

Part 1

'How sharper than a serpent's tooth it is
to have a thankless child!'
William Shakespeare, *King Lear*

For a long time – she didn't know how long – there had been nothing. A kind of dream-nothing that she floated in; a mist that sometimes receded and showed the edges of the world. But still, she was
not in the world. She made what brief contact was required, and then
she was back in the nothing place.

The nothing place needs no thought: it is an eternal now. Balanced
between past and future, here there is no colour. No sound. It's like
being wrapped in cotton wool, except there is no sensation of softness. It is neither comforting, nor terrifying. She doesn't know how
long she's been here. It has been a long time.

Somewhere out there is life – but she has been here for so long it
seems that she doesn't remember the other place, the route back. It is
lost in the mists sometime. That's the place where her body is, but she
doesn't need it any more. It's fine here.

She doesn't think, and she doesn't know. But she dreams.

The dreams are tiny moments; pearls on a wire. She cannot tell if
they are memories or constructions. Fragments from her childhood:
the joy of a sketch perfectly executed; opening her lunchbox to find
her favourite kind of plum; smiling up at eyes that were smiling
down; lighting the New Year candles. Were these moments in her
life that she's returning to?

There are other dreams, other memories.

Is that her signing the marriage register? Crying with the pain of
labour? Holding that pillow, sick with the knowledge of what came
next? She learns to tell when they are coming and dives back into the
mist. They're part of him, of them, of those two men in her life that
she's in flight from. Her husband. Her son.

She likes it best when there is nothing, when she is floating bodiless
in a void of her own making, a place where there are no demands on
her time, or on her emotions. She is swimming in an endless sea. She
can be free there.

One minute she was there in the mist – and the next everything was collapsing around her. The world was shaking. From inside cupboards dusty boxes that hadn't seen the light of day for months came crashing down – their contents striking her, pulling her back into the world. She pulled the covers over her head to protect herself, and lay on the bed, curled up. Slowly she let her ears pick out sounds from the general chaos. Outside the apartment block she could hear, hardly muffled, a colossal grinding and rumbling, and beneath it, the sound of human screams. Earthquake! Sirens wailed a warning, 'Get out! Get out! Get out!'

She ran into the other room. Here too everything was in disorder, all of the small elements of life tossed around as though by a giant child in a tantrum. The child! He wasn't there. And where was Harry? Had he gone running again? The baby-sling swung crazily on its hook, near the empty bouncer. She turned to the door.

And that was when everything collapsed. She was engulfed in cold black water. She was blind and breathless. She was barely aware of objects hitting her as she clawed for air – no sense of up or down. And then everything was dark and she knew no more.

It wasn't that strange, someone running. Everyone was running, screaming, crouching on the ground, with arms held over their heads. The warning siren wailed and aftershocks still rocked the earth. I didn't trust myself to keep my feet, but I had to get away.

In the distance, faster than seemed possible, a black wall of water was creeping up the streets of Taro. Boats and bits of wood floated on its crest and splintered buildings screamed in protest as it passed. I had a head start – I could outrun it. This would be my only chance to save myself – to actually save my life. I lengthened my stride, feeling the pleasurable burn of warming muscles.

Soon I had run right out of town, following the road that wound up through the mountains. I was heading inland, to the forested areas where nature was left to go her own way, and casual visitors were rare.

I stopped to catch my breath. I was used to running. That had been a constant in my life – when everything went wrong, I could go running, and rejoice in the physical control I had over my body: the speed, the freedom. I knew I could get a long way if I could only pace myself.

What had happened back there? Living in Japan I had grown used to tremors, and the constant grumblings of the continental plates. But this was different – this was really big – as big as the Hanshin quake of '95 at least. The giant waves that had destroyed the town had surely caused more far-reaching destruction. All change again! With a quake of that magnitude, there would be strong aftershocks for days. If there was going to be any more of that, I wanted to be on higher ground.

The earthquake hadn't been part of my plans – but, having made the decision to leave, it had provided the perfect cover.

But I'm getting ahead of myself.

I had decided to abandon her on a grey afternoon in March. I considered telling her, making one last attempt to fix things. But when I went into our bedroom she lay with her face to the wall, as she had for weeks. Her eyes were closed. I waited a long moment before starting to pack.

I had been stockpiling foodstuffs, warm clothes and bedding for weeks already, in a little shack that I had stumbled across on one of my regular runs, but at this time of year the cold would be the biggest issue. I pulled on a warm parka and waterproof trousers and threw my notebooks, pens and a few snacks into a small satchel, and turned to look at her one last time. There was no sign that she was aware of the world at all.

Then, beneath my feet, the floor had begun to shake. I fell. I remember striking my head. All around me plates were falling from shelves and smashing; pictures flew from the walls. I wanted to get out, but I couldn't stay on my feet. I grabbed whatever handholds I could find, and made it out onto the street.

There had been screaming and a loud grinding, rumbling noise, then a deafening roar that sounded like a thousand airplanes. Earthquake? I didn't immediately make the connection, but then it clicked. We were near the sea. Tsunami.

For several long moments I considered going back into the house, to try to stir my wife. But it was too late. She would not respond. I could not get through. Sirens began to wail, sounding the warning. It was 3.51pm. I turned my face inland and started running in earnest.

Before long I found myself in the forest, with a quiet hiking track stretched out before me. It was very quiet, and glancing at my watch I saw it was only 4.30pm. It hadn't taken me long to leave the chaos behind.

I looked back down the path I had taken, a path that had started behind the cemetery at the edge of town. It was a regular run – I knew where it went – soon it would join up with the hiking trails of the local nature preserve, a place I had escaped to regularly since we had moved north. The land rose sharply from the coast, and was heavily forested. Further inland, where the crags were highest, the restricted zone started, and just inside this zone I had discovered an abandoned shack some months before.

In that small, dilapidated retreat in the woods I could think straight, away from the life that had become intolerable to me. So far I had rarely stayed overnight; guilt had always dragged me back to family life, to her and the child; but the peace had come to seem more and more seductive. Bringing cans and noodles and other imperishable foodstuffs had come to seem like insurance for the future, for the moment I chose to disappear. I had squirrelled away several caches in case one or more of them were discovered. I had always been planning on leaving, but it was a question of when.

Sachiko woke up, and realised she wasn't in her own bed. Then she remembered, and the pain hit her at the same time. Her ribs were the worst; it hurt to breathe. She could feel bandages around them. A dull pain pounded in her head and her thoughts were slow, as though she had been sedated. So she had survived then.

Everything felt very uncertain, but she remembered the shaking – and then the black wall of water that the world had become, and then nothing. *But I'm alive!*

Sachiko lay quietly, taking stock of the sounds around her. She realised that she wasn't alone. The futon she lay on was one of many crammed into a space she gradually recognised as part of the local shrine. It was dark now, apart from a small night light on the other side of the room. All around her people were sleeping, muffled against the cold night with blankets and surrounded by bundles of rescued belongings. It was too dark to make out faces. She could hear nothing but the regular sounds of breathing, of people sleeping deeply. What had become of her home? If she had survived, did that mean that Harry had too?

There was no one to ask, and she felt too weak to try to rouse anyone. All she could do for now was sleep, build up her strength and hope for the best in the morning. She closed her eyes again and tried to let sleep take her. For weeks she had hidden in dreams, but now they wouldn't come. She thought about Tashi.

He had arrived in the coldest hour before dawn – cut out after a hard labour that could have no happy ending the natural way. They had wanted it to be natural, but she was too narrow. The first failure.

He was put in a glass case, with all his needs catered for, and she lay in a hospital bed feeling the raw wound, and the savage after-pains. All around her were other women – it was a ward of eight – with their new babies. She could hear soft gurgles and coos, occasionally a cry, cut off as a breast was offered. That was the second failure. Tashi would not take to her breast. The midwives were kind and spent hours showing her the correct latch – but Tashi wouldn't open his mouth: he just set it in a line. They tried to show her how to open it with a knuckle, and slip the nipple in behind, but she couldn't get the hang of it. Or he wouldn't countenance it; anyway, whichever it was, Tashi ended up being fed by bottle. At first with expressed milk, and then (oh the sympathetic looks of the other mothers!) with formula, as Sachiko's milk inevitably dried up.

Feeding Tashi by bottle was no easy task. He wouldn't take the milk, and sobbed with frustrated hunger, or would gulp it, then scream for hours with colic. She couldn't get a handle on what caused his sudden cries. The nurses said he would grow out of it. After a little while they pronounced her all better and sent her home with her new baby.

Harry tried to help, but he was often at work and Sachiko was left to fill the empty hours. That was when she began to experiment with absenting herself from the here and now. When it seemed there was nothing more she could do for Tashi she went into her nothing place. She ensured he was clean and dry, fed him whatever he would take, and then she left.

The neighbours heard the child of course – his cries through the thin walls had become a backdrop to their nights. Most worked in the daytime though. No one went to call on the new mother and child; it was considered a time for privacy. If they had, they would have seen her curled up on the bed whilst Tashi lay in his cot and wailed, with Sachiko hidden in a little room that she made in her mind. The nothing place was her refuge. She played with the space to make it feel like hers, to make her feel safe. She could make it look like anything! At first it was just like a normal room, with a door – she could leave any time. But after a while, when she opened that door there was only a mist – and she began to be afraid that she was lost.

Eventually, morning came. At some point Sachiko had fallen into a restless sleep, and when she woke the next time she found people stirring around her. Some beds were already empty. Chinks of light showed through the wooden shutters. The painkillers had worn off, and the mild respite that they had offered was replaced by a raging thirst.

Her head hurt, and when she put her hand up she felt a bandage holding a thick pad onto the back of her head. She sat up, wincing at the pain in her ribs – it felt like at least one of them was cracked. No one took any notice of her for now. She discovered that she was lightly dressed in nightclothes – not hers. Her feet were clad in mismatched socks, again not hers.

Getting up she hobbled over to the door. Opening it, she found an assortment of plastic sandals on the wooden porch, and slid her feet into a pair. It was light outside, but the flat white of the sky made it hard to tell the time.

The little shrine sat amidst the trees, tucked into the mountainside. A muddy, leaf-strewn path and a steep flight of steps connected it to the town, and behind it the cemetery spread out over a number of stepped plots that petered out into thick tree cover. Around the shrine were several stone benches, one of which was occupied by two women who seemed familiar, one young and the other old.

Looking up, the younger woman smiled at her.

'Oh – you're awake! The doctor was worried that you'd got a terrible concussion from that blow to the head. How are you feeling?'

'I do have a headache, but I'm sure there must be others worse off than me. Thank you so much for asking. I need to find out what's happened to my family. An English man, and a baby boy. Do you know if they're here too?'

'Of course, I remember your family. And you are Sachiko, *ne*? This is my mother, Aikiko, and I'm Hiroko. I'm sorry, but I haven't seen them. It's been chaos. All of the men are out searching for survivors – the whole seafront is washed away. The town hall is gone, and the *onsen*, and most of the main street. The railway is out too. And the power.'

Sachiko felt a cold shiver of fear course through her. It felt all too real after the months of drifting, but at the same time had the quality of a nightmare. Her legs felt weak, and she would have stumbled, but Hiroko, with instinctive kindness, had already sprung up to help her to a seat. Pictures came into her head, and suddenly Sachiko could place her. She worked in one of the village shops and always had a ready smile. Her husband was a stocky man – the kind of man you couldn't picture without work clothes on. Now she looked terribly worried, and tired.

Sachiko remembered she had a child – a toddler of three or four. There was no sign of him either.

'Is your son ok?'

'Luckily he was found – he turned up on the roof of the school. The school caretaker was able to pick him and the other children up and take them to safety, but in the confusion he couldn't contact me here to tell me he was safe. I just found out an hour ago, and I'm waiting for him now.'

Sachiko tried to feel thankful for her.

'You must be so relieved.'

'I'm sure your family will turn up too – your husband is probably just somewhere safe with the child and can't get in touch with you. People are turning up all the time. You need to keep your strength up, so you can look after them when they're found. There's some food inside if you want to get some breakfast?'

Sachiko wasn't so sure that Hiroko was right. She had a presentiment of doom, as though a part of her knew she would never see them again. Automatically she hid her feelings, and tried to inject a little lightness into her tone.

'Thanks – I do need to eat. I won't do them any good if I make myself ill and can't look after them when they're found.'

'That's the spirit. Come on – I'll show you where the food is. Will you be ok here for the moment, Mama?'

The old woman had been nodding off whilst they spoke, but woke when her name was mentioned.

'What? What was that?'

'Mama, I'm going to take Sachiko and show her where to get some breakfast. Would you like to come and have a lie-down inside?'

'Is there no word of Kaito?' Her voice quavered, and she seemed almost at the end of her strength. Hiroko's reply was gentle.

'Not yet, Mama – I'm sure it won't be much longer. Why don't you sleep a little?'

Now Sachiko remembered the older woman's husband – a quiet-voiced fisherman she had seen occasionally, bringing his catches into the shop. Hiroko went inside and got the old lady settled. When she came back outside she was carrying a bowl of rice for Sachiko.

'Sorry, it's pretty basic. Hopefully some extra supplies will be coming in soon. There hasn't been much news, but it sounds like the whole coast got it.'

'What happened?'

'They are saying an earthquake out at sea triggered a massive tsunami. I've never heard of one this big though. The sea walls are supposed to stop it reaching the town.'

They were silent for a while. Sachiko picked at her rice and wished she had some seasoning, or a few pickles to relieve its blandness. A little *daikon*, or some sour plums. Then she told herself off, sternly, for being so selfish. She was lucky to have food. She had little appetite, but made herself eat anyway.

She was pushing the last few grains of rice around with her chopsticks when Hiroko came to collect the bowl. Her eyes were full of concern as she took it from her.

'Sachiko, you still look very pale. Why don't you go and lie down again for a bit? I'll come and wake you immediately if I hear anything. You should get some rest and try not to worry so much. There's nothing you can do for now.'

'You're right, Hiroko. I do feel tired. If you're sure there's nothing I can do to help?'

'Nothing except make yourself better. Off you go now.'

Sachiko made her way back to the futon where she had awoken earlier and lay down. She closed her eyes and tried to sleep.

She kept remembering the empty house. Harry had not been home before the tsunami had struck. The time before that was hazy; she couldn't separate what she had dreamed from what was real. She felt that if only she could remember she would know what had happened to him, and where Tashi was.

四

Sachiko hadn't been able to sleep for long. She tried to help in the makeshift kitchen that had been set up to feed the survivors. There were dozens of people shoehorned into the shrine – many of them injured. Hiroko was busy tending to their needs and Sachiko didn't like to bother her with questions. There had been several thousand people living in Taro. There must be more people elsewhere, the school where Hiroko's son was, for example. She tried to picture the layout of the town. There must be other places on high ground where survivors would be taken. Had everything at sea level been destroyed?

Hiroko had mentioned that there were men out looking for survivors, and that it was part of a massive earthquake that had hit the whole north-eastern coast of Honshu. Looking around she couldn't see anyone using their phone – this was so unusual that it must mean that both power and phone networks were still out. She wondered where Hiroko had got her news. Was there someone with a working radio?

Just then she felt the ground buck beneath her. Her first instinct was to get out in the open as fast as possible, but she forced herself to be calm. Around her sleepers awoke, stumbled, and fled the enclosure of four walls. She saw Hiroko's mother Aikiko struggling to her feet and ran to help her.

'I'm ok – don't worry about me, Sachiko. You should try to save yourself. I'm an old woman, and I've been through many earth tremors in my time. Go! Shoo!'

Sachiko reached out and gently took her by the arm.

'Even if it's just an aftershock it can still be dangerous. Come – we'll go outside together and I can find Hiroko for you.'

The old woman looked stubborn, but allowed herself to be led outside. The little clearing next to the shrine soon became crowded as more and more people awoke and fled the shelter. In the distance Sachiko could hear rocks tumbling down the slope, but there was no more shaking, and after a little while the air began to be filled with the sound of birdsong. Of course – after such a major quake there were bound to be aftershocks. It would likely be weeks until they stopped.

After a while, when it seemed as though everything was still again, people started to filter back inside. Sachiko made Aikiko comfortable. All around her people were settling down to sleep or staring despondently into space. It felt as though there was nothing to do but wait. And Sachiko was done with waiting.

She decided to go and search for her family herself. There had been no news of them, but some survivors were still being dug out from the rubble. Maybe if she went back to their building she could find a clue as to where they had gone, what had become of them. Harry would go there too, to search for her, if he were still alive. Either way, it was better than sitting here, knowing nothing, doing nothing.

As she climbed down the steps from the shrine where the survivors had taken refuge the ground began to tremble with another aftershock. She paused and held onto the rail, wondering if what she was doing was wise. The tremor was short lived – only a few seconds. She decided to go on. She descended the few remaining steps to the roadway, and followed it the short distance to the village.

It took her many minutes to orient herself in the main street. Everything was in the wrong place, messy. She tried to make some pattern out of the chaos – splintered wood and stone, cars crushed and cast about as if someone had picked up the land like a carpet and given it a shake. Here and there a structure remained standing, one house seemingly anchored to the earth by the fishing boat that rested at a crazy angle on its roof. Eventually she located the remains of their building. The small prefabs had been levelled utterly by the fury of the waves, until nothing but the foundations remained to hint at what had once been a home.

Odd things seemed to have come through the disaster unscathed – a child's schoolbag rested, clean, on a pile of shattered wood. Near it a teddy bear and some flowers formed an offering to the departed. Underneath her feet, the crunch of shattered glass; dozens of photographs, books, letters – mud-stained and all but illegible.

It seemed a miracle that she had been pulled alive from the mess, with nothing but a bump on the head, sore ribs and some minor scrapes to show for her ordeal. The roof of the building had been ripped off, and lay some 100 metres away. With a shock she saw Tashi's bouncer, the fabric stained and ripped, but the frame intact. Gradually, more familiar items appeared, as if clarified from the general chaos – items of clothing, odd chopsticks, fragments of china bearing remembered patterns.

She knelt carefully and began to sift through the rubbish, searching for she knew not what, the grey sky pressing on her, shutting her in with the immensity of their loss. There were no clues here to what had become of her family – unless they lay buried beneath the rubble; but it didn't seem deep enough for anyone to be trapped underneath. She listened, but the morning was silent. In the distance, striking in their red hazard suits, members of the volunteer fire corps continued to search for bodies. As they completed each quarter, they left markers to show where they had been, and looking around Sachiko could see similar markers. It looked like the area had already been combed thoroughly.

She didn't know why she had come. Maybe just to prove to herself that they were really gone, that they were nowhere to be found. To start the process of grieving.

She closed her eyes and bowed her head, feeling a swelling misery that filled her until she thought her heart would burst. It was as if she hadn't known how much she loved Tashi until that moment; as if her love for him had been masked by the months of distance, of isolation, and now the mist had been swept aside to make room for grief such as she had never known. She realised that she was crying, feeling the tears coursing down her face, her breath coming in gasps. She had never realised that grieving could be so profoundly physical. A part of her had hoped that they would be found, and she had clung onto that thought; but looking at the devastation around her she felt the knowledge that they were lost forever settle into her brain like a key into a lock.

Suddenly the ground began to shake again and she heard shouts from the red-suited figures in the distance. She looked over to where they were and saw that they had dropped to the ground, and were barely visible amidst the wreckage. She couldn't summon the energy to protect herself. Everything seemed pointless now – the journey back to humanity a mountain that she could never climb.

I reached my hideout just as the sun went down completely, and left the little clearing in darkness. I unhooked the door of the little one-room cabin and peered in. It was silent, and, as far as I could tell, exactly as I had left it. The single wooden shutter was still fastened; the torn ricepaper blinds drawn. I switched on my torch and played it around the small space. It didn't look like anything, human or animal, had disturbed the bedding or the things I had left there. I dumped my bag on the floor and breathed a sigh of relief. Now I could relax.

I had left oil for the lantern on one of my previous visits, and the first thing I did was to fill it and light the wick. The little cabin was immediately filled with a cosy glow. It was unlikely that anyone would be passing, to see a chink of light through the window, but I quickly draped a jumper over it, just in case. The rest of the cabin was pretty well insulated; I didn't think much light would escape.

I was famished; eating was my next priority. One of the things I've always loved about living in Japan is the sheer variety of foods that can be freeze dried and preserved. Within minutes I was tucking into a bowl of instant ramen; the thick noodles swimming in a hot tasty broth. As I ate, slurping up the noodles, I considered my options. I could stay here for weeks – especially if I could supplement the food I had stashed away with some hunting or fishing. I had come to the point where running away to some quiet place, to be by myself, seemed like the only thing to do. I could have returned to England, but what would I have done there? I had well and truly burned my bridges when I left. They say you choose your friends but the devil chooses your relations – and bereavement is sadly an excellent way of seeing where you really stand. So, I had left my job, what remained of my family, and everyone I had known, and fled to Japan. I had told myself I was following a dream: I would write the book that I had always known was within me. But of course, life intervened. Living the life of a family man, bringing in the wages, had seen that dream receding ever further over the horizon. And, gradually, I realised that

I wasn't ready to give it up yet. I needed to give myself the space to see if I still had the ability to make it real. Everyone needs a place to think, after all.

I didn't sleep well last night. I was plagued by bad dreams. I was running through dark city streets calling for Sachiko. I knew she was somewhere in front of me – I kept catching glimpses of someone I was sure was her, but I couldn't catch up with her. There was a feeling of menace, and several times I woke up and tried to clear my head, limbs stiff from the cold. Each time I fell into sleep again the dream continued, and a nameless terror haunted me during the brief waking moments in between.

When I woke up I was chilled to the bone; my chest tight. It's much colder up here in the mountains. I made myself a hot cup of tea, and sat, clutching the warm cup and eating nuts, and considered the day that stretched out before me. I willed myself not to think about them. It's like they've followed me here, like even now they're hunting me, blocking me, distracting me. My thoughts scatter. I try to regroup. I've come here to write. I have no shortage of pens or paper, but I want to get everything straight in my head first.

Another cup of tea. I catch my mind drifting back to the first time we met. She was so demure, but with a mutinous sparkle in her eye. She laughed at my jokes. I longed to touch her hair – it looked so soft. I took her number. We promised to meet again. Did meet again. We discovered her country through each other's eyes.

But that's not the story I want to write. It's not about me. I came to this far land, away from everything I'd ever known, precisely because I didn't want to write about me, but about an 'other': about the myths and legends and ghosts that populate Japan; the spirit realm that is never far away.

More memories. Of the way she retreated from me, gradually, as if she were vanishing into the distance even though we inhabited the same house. Of the child that seemed less and less my own. I can't fight them any more. I relax and let the memories take me. After all I'm safe here.

六

'How much rice do you think we'll need today, Hiroko?'

'Oh, a few new people came in yesterday. I think we'll need at least two and a half kilos.'

Sachiko measured out the rice and Hiroko helped her carry it over to the sink. They had been moved to a refuge centre in the nearby city of Kuji, and for the last several mornings she had been helping Hiroko prepare what felt like industrial amounts of rice to feed the growing population of refugees from the coast. It helped to distract her from the lack of news, and it felt good to be doing something useful.

'We're lucky today – we've got eggs as well – and some rice seasoning. We'll be able to make a nice breakfast.'

That was just like Hiroko – she always seemed to be able to find the bright side in any situation. It was a relief for Sachiko to let her take the lead.

'What do you think we should do with them?'

'Well, we could make some omelette. In fact, there's quite a few supplies starting to be delivered now. I saw rice seasoning, *daikon* – even a bit of tofu and some seasoned plums. I think we should get the rice cooking, and then we can plan what to do next. Of course it will be a stretch with so many people.'

'How many do you think there are here now?'

'I counted 128 mouths to feed last night – including kids, but not babies. There should be a few more people along to help soon I think.'

They were using the sink in the school kitchen to wash the rice, but, as there still wasn't any running water, Sachiko was turning the rice while Hiroko poured water over it from one of a row of buckets that had been left there earlier.

'It feels like we've gone back to the old times, washing the rice this way. I'm so used to setting the rice cooker I had to ask Mama about how much water to use, and how long to cook it. Can you imagine? Luckily Mama knows all about such things. It's not so strange to her, doing things the old way.'

Hiroko was doing her best to be cheerful, but in fact both of them were trying to distract themselves. There wasn't much news to punctuate the waiting, although every able-bodied man was out looking for survivors. It did little good. Few bodies had been recovered from the wreckage after the first 48 hours, and none alive.

In the background, the radio murmured with a news report. Briefly tuning in Sachiko realised it was a recap of news she had already heard. The announcer was describing the aftermath of the series of giant waves that had followed the earthquake, travelling several miles inland, smashing everything in their path. The destruction had been almost total. Aftershocks followed the waves at unpredictable intervals; strong tremors that continued to test the resolve of the survivors and completed the destruction of already-damaged buildings. It seemed that these would go on for weeks. Sachiko still couldn't believe that she had made it through; a piece of luck that felt ironic indeed given her withdrawal from a world she felt unequal to.

Sachiko went down to the makeshift morgue that had been set up, and saw the bodies of the dead laid out in their dozens. There was still no sign of her family – it was as if they had both entirely vanished. No one had seen a *gaijin* with a baby; no trace of their bodies had been uncovered. It was just possible that they had been washed out to sea. Tens of thousands were still missing; thousands more would probably never be found. The fire corps were excavating the thick mud that covered those structures still standing, masked against the stench of rotting fish, deposited in the most unlikely places by the hungry waves. Taro had defences against the sea, against the tsunami that were not uncommon here on the edge of the Pacific. But there had never been an earthquake like this. They were calling it a, 'megathrust event'. Such inadequate words to describe the shattering of worlds.

Hiroko broke into the dark spell cast by the news.

'I'm sure that's the same report I listened to earlier. Come on – it doesn't seem like there's any point dwelling on what we can't change. They'll only tell us what they think we need to know anyway. We might as well make some omelette whilst we wait for the rice to cook. Did you get a chance to count the eggs?'

Sachiko shook her head.

'Sorry, Hiroko – I completely forgot. I can't seem to keep anything in my brain for more than two minutes. I keep seeing all those bodies in the morgue. And it's like the news never changes – the same bare facts, again and again, as if they're drip-feeding us as little as they can get away with.'

'Well, there's nothing you can do about it, Sachiko. You've done all you can for now. And everybody knows that the best way to stop worrying is to keep busy. Once we've finished preparing lunch, let's go and do some more sorting, ok?'

'You're right, Hiroko. You're always so practical. I don't know how you do it. I feel so lost.'

'We're all lost, Sachiko, and afraid. I'm scared silly. I don't know what the future holds. All I know is that it will be hard. We will have to build everything again. Everything! And I'm not sure that will even be possible everywhere, but we have to start somewhere. And we might as well start right now, don't you think? Now go and tell me how many eggs there are, and then see if you can find any dried fish in the relief crates. We can't move mountains, but at least we can make sure that people eat well.'

There was still no sign of her family. Every day Sachiko waited her turn at the Internet terminal – scouring the lists of those rescued. She had left descriptions of them both with the authorities, and they alerted her to the tiny percentage of *gaijin* that had been recovered. Each time she pulled back the sheet from a face, surrounded by dark curls, her heart froze; it was never him. Caucasian male, 6 foot 2 inches. Dark hair. Blue eyes. There was so much left out – could that really describe him? There were very few babies.

So she lived in limbo – one day hoping and believing that they were still alive and looking for her too, then the next convinced that she would never see them again. And, after all, in a country of more than a million displaced, it would be like looking for a single petal in a heap of cherry blossom.

Now she couldn't stand the atmosphere of the refugee centre any more. She had to break the cycle of listening to news that never changed. She decided to go for a walk.

The spring days were still cool, and the air felt chilly as she wandered down the streets at random, heading towards the edge of town. Here the lanes were narrow – and the buildings, one- and two-storey, opened straight onto the road. As she passed each home she caught glimpses of a disconcerting normality – it was as if the whole nightmare had never happened. On the streets there were still traces of the earthquake, the start of the clean-up operation – but these small dwellings in the lanes had come through relatively unscathed, and their owners had been quick to mend and sweep and return their lives to normality as fast as possible. There were baskets hanging from the low eves, spilling out ivy, with spring flowers peeping from the tops. Potted plants lined the lane, with green spears of buds poking through the soil. Above, the thin slice of blue sky showed scudding clouds. Sachiko hadn't noticed any of these things for a long time. She had been too lost inside herself, in the room that she had created in her mind. But now these and other impressions of the real world came flooding in. She felt something inside herself straining into life; as though she were a spring bulb with new shoots blindly questing towards the light.

Turning a corner she came upon a prayer gate, red paint flaking. Uneven steps snaked up to the Shinto shrine that was almost hidden amongst the tall trees that surrounded it. She placed her foot upon the first step, the call of a wild place strong. The quietness of these city streets didn't fit reality; the absurd destruction of so many lives.

It had been one of the very first things that she had loved about Harry – his fascination for the wild. He had an infallible sense of direction, as though he had a built-in map. Early in their relationship they would go walking in the mountains together, and they never got lost. If he'd once visited a place, he would remember all its ways and paths forever more. She often joked he was like the mountain men in the old stories, only happy when he was amidst his beloved peaks. Those walks together, discovering new places, were amongst their best times. The wilderness had been the side of Japan that Harry had loved, especially as he railed against the formality, rules and regulations that allowed the Japanese to live harmoniously together. Perhaps it was when he started to go walking alone that they had begun to drift apart.

It had been a very long time since she had visited a shrine – not since she discovered that she was pregnant with Tashi. She had felt strange about it then. After all, hadn't she left all that behind when she had married Harry and embraced his world? Maybe she had already started to understand it wouldn't work between them, that it was time to start trying to reconnect with her own culture. And there was a comfort in prayer.

The steps were steep and uneven; the thin rope that snaked up along the side was small reassurance in the face of their vertiginous height. Soon she had lost sight of the streets behind her completely, and the only sounds were the wind and the cawing of crows. Fallen leaves rotted by the snows of winter muffled her steps, save for the occasional crack of branches that littered the steps. As she climbed, the trees grew ever larger; native cedars replaced the fir trees that marched in military lines across so much of the landscape. Sunlight slanted through branches that were starting to be covered with the raiment of spring. Above her she could see another gate; she was nearing the shrine and the smell of incense lay heavy on the air. Stopping at the burners, she purified herself with the smoke that drifted from them, and rang the bell that would inform the spirits someone had come to worship. The very familiarity of the actions was comforting; it felt like she was coming back to her true self, before she had denied her heritage. She moved into the shrine proper, and was relieved to see that it was deserted. She had the place to herself.

Climbing the steps she threw a few yen into the *saisen-bako*, and then stepped back, bowing and clapping as custom demanded. The ritual was relaxing, even though the rational part of her mind, the part that had married Harry, was not sure that it would make the slightest bit of difference. She considered what to pray for. Should she ask for her family to be returned safely? Would that be a wasted prayer? It seemed certain that they had both perished when Taro was destroyed. Maybe she should save her prayers for Japan, or for the thousands of children orphaned by the 'Great East Japan Earthquake' as it had started to be called, or for those affected by the radiation even now leaking into the sea and the air. What future would they have?

In the end she found she couldn't decide what to pray for; there seemed so many vying demands, so many broken lives. All she could hope for was that the future would bring something better. She sent an inchoate wish to the universe to make it so. Surely between destruction and salvation there should be some balance?

She rang the temple bell again and backed away respectfully from the shrine. She would have liked to stay in this peaceful place a little while longer, savouring the whisper of the breeze amidst the trees and listening to the birds complaining of their little ills. She turned her feet back to the refugee centre, descending the steep steps with care. She had nowhere else to go, and maybe she could be of some use there.

七

I keep having flashbacks so intense they have the quality of a hallucination. I couldn't tell you quite what triggers them, or whether they're connected to Tashi. I'm trying to stay rational, but events keep betraying me. I can't tell what's true any more.

Everything is fragmented – like I've been slipping in and out of a fugue state. I am awake, but not in my body; I am travelling, yet standing still, jumping between episodes and stories of my life, and then losing all memory of them. Between these fugues, I am back in the cabin, aware of time passing. Ravenously, I snatch a bite to eat and then go travelling again. And then I am back in the moments before I fled Taro, reliving them. It is nothing like a dream, unless you've ever had a dream where you could feel pain and smell the characteristic scents of familiar places. I am there and forced to live every moment again... I am another 'I', not me... I am lost in the past, trapped in my memories, living those first days with Tashi again.

Somewhere on the edge of a scream, ululating, piercing, angry, ragged; I cannot call it crying. It seems more a shout of rage at the universe, at this place, at me. I wish he would stop.

I turn my face to the wall, and put my fingers in my ears like a child, and I wish he would stop. Like an air raid siren, it leaves me on the edge of panic. Urgently, he broadcasts the constant subtext, 'Danger! Danger! Run! Escape!' But where can I run to? This is my life. This is my son. This has been my reality for...

Has it been three months since he was born? Only three months? Three whole months? The screaming goes on. It scatters my thoughts. It fragments my 'I' until I can't tell where I am, when I am. I can't remember the last time I slept. Or the last time I spoke to another human being.

I realise I am crouched down, foetal, rocking in the corner. Like a crazy person!

I look over, at the baby bouncer, at the red-faced, screaming creature. At the child. My child? I don't know any more. I could swear that from between

the narrowed lids – lost in folds of creased red flesh – an intelligence is look-
ing at me. Measuring me.

Could it be? I heard whispers of changelings, children swapped by malev-
olent faerie beings. I hear voices outside my head, from far away, and echoing
as though the speakers were in a chamber of steel.

Everything has changed. Nothing will ever be the same again. I had been
a writer, and she had been happy, and we had moved here, to this small fish-
ing town, on the coast of north-eastern Japan, full of dreams, with a new job,
ready to embrace a new life.

And now he is here. And everything has changed. She doesn't speak any
more. Day after day she turns her head to the wall, dull-eyed, saying noth-
ing, in her own private world; a place I can't visit. I ask her what's wrong,
but she doesn't answer my questions. Soon the questions become demands, I
goad her, beg her to respond in some way, to engage with me, to engage with
her child. Day after day that creature screams and shits and vomits and eats
up all my energy and dreams. And grows – as if these are all the food it
needs.

I am filled with rage. This is not why I came here. Somewhere beneath a
pile of marking and nappies lies the book that I started, so full of optimism.
The screams echo around our tiny kitchen and I can't think; can't even
remember the narrative that had been crystal clear, ready to unfurl like a
flower, the chapters that had been fully realised in my mind; the work of
genius just waiting to be committed to paper.

I try to keep a record of the days, of the hours, of the weeks, of the months
passing. A life punctuated by tantrums. I go through to the bedroom of our
tiny two tatami apartment to look for my notebook.

I think the screaming started just before 6.30am – but I can't be sure. Had
I been asleep? These days I often find myself lying tensed and awake, lis-
tening for screams even when it is silent. Sachiko just lies there, ignoring me.
From time to time she gets up, and drags herself to the bathroom. She doesn't
wash – just uses the toilet facilities. If I leave water, she will drink it. At first
it was the same with food, but lately she has taken to ignoring it. I can see
the bones jutting out through her chest where once there were breasts.

Some outside agency must have done this to her, to us. We have travelled so far from what a normal family should be that I can only believe some external power is responsible.

She is awake, I think. Her eyes are open. I try to catch her gaze, but she just looks right through me. I don't exist.

If we were home, in my old home of England, before I came here to this land of islands and mountains, I would take her to someone – try to find out what is wrong. But there is no one like that here in this tiny place. They don't have doctors for the mind at the local clinic. And, anyway, it would never do, to speak of mental collapse. Crime and madness are too closely intertwined in people's minds.

Maybe it's because of the sedatives that the doctors prescribe her. She seems drugged, slow; and as the days pass I feel her travelling away from me. Now she is never there at all.

Beside the bed lies my notebook. It is worn and dog-eared, and lately has turned from a repository for my dreams into a simple log. Feeding. Changing. Hours slept. Hours spent lying awake listening to the screaming, the silence. I make the entry, and with it confirm my resolve to be free.

As if reaching the end of a film reel, I snapped back into the present. It was pitch black inside the cabin, and I felt my way over to the door. I opened it. Outside was a moonless dark that made the forest outside my little clearing seem more impenetrable than ever. I was alone. I strained my ears, listening for any sound in the night, any indication that I wasn't entirely alone in the world; the night was silent, but for a faint breeze that made me shiver. I went back inside and crawled into my sleeping bag. I thought about the strange, fragmented memories. They felt real, but didn't quite match up with what I thought I remembered. It's as if the past was rewriting itself. My head hurt from the effort of trying to mesh mismatched realities together, and I was as exhausted as if I'd run a full marathon. Soon I fell into a dreamless sleep.

八

There were a surprising amount of children in the refuge centre – Sachiko wondered why she hadn't noticed before how many children there were in Taro; but then she hadn't really ever taken part in the community of the place. Now their cries sounded from behind partitions. Everyone was afraid of nuclear contamination from the shattered reactors at the Fukushima power plant just down the coast, so they were not allowed to play outside, and there were constantly children underfoot playing complicated games of chase and hide. Sachiko thought about Tashi – it was like he was receding into a haze, and she couldn't quite bring his features to mind. What could she remember about him?

He had just learned to roll over. When she cleaned him, rubbing his smooth skin with almond oil, she found a strange waxy substance in the folds of his skin – beneath his chin and in the creases at the top of his thighs. He wasn't a chubby baby; it had taken him three months to grow into his newborn clothes. His skin was blue white, and his eyes too round for pure Japanese. You could see the European in him. His wispy black hair had a curl to it that echoed Harry's.

He had never smiled. When they weren't creased in a face red with screaming, his eyes were a milky blue, like all newborns. Now she would never know what colour they would have been. She had no photographs of him – she hadn't sent any to her parents when he was born.

With a shock she realised that it had been almost three years since she had even spoken with her parents. She had tried to avoid thinking about them. She wondered what they had made of the earthquake, and felt a pang that she had not sent any word to them since then. Had they even looked for her? At some point they had stopped being a family it seemed. When had that occurred?

Sachiko had not precisely argued with her parents – there had never been any raised voices – she had just gradually stopped going to see them. They were of the old traditional school, and she was on an ever-

31

westward trajectory. For some time she had continued to make the annual journey to Osaka to celebrate *Obon*, the festival of the dead, with them, but visits in between had tailed off. And after the first time she had taken Harry with her as her fiancé, and the meeting had been so stilted that she had been embarrassed both for her parents and the man she was planning to marry, she had resolved to cut herself off from them, and the conventional life that they had planned, and start afresh.

She had always been a good girl. She had worked hard to get into the right school and pulled her weight for the team.

Her father had been a salaryman for Mitsubishi. She had never been close to him. He was always working late, and when he finally came home she would be banished to her bedroom whilst he ate alone, served by her mother. She had always been a little frightened of him, although he had never once raised his voice to her, or to her mother. She thought maybe their relationship would have been better if she had been born a boy.

Sachiko's memories of her mother were more complicated. There had always been an emotional distance between them. Her love was shown but never spoken. It was there – in the beautifully arranged lunchboxes that contained her favourite foods and the way she silently provided for all her daughter's needs. Her father's love had been there too, in his quiet pride when she had got a place at a good university. She could see that now, but she had become blind to it in her infatuation with Harry. At some point her parents, and all they stood for, had come to seem monstrous to her. Was it their politics? Of course they were conservative to the core, but Sachiko had never been political. At university she had mostly focussed on her studies, and ignored the feminists and socialists and anything else with a whiff of the radical.

Harry made it easy to turn her back on her past. She remembered their early dates. It wasn't so much the jazz and western books – they were common enough in a metropolis such as Tokyo. It was his sense of humour – so different from the Japanese. He was brash but subtle, a mass of contradictions. And if Japanese people seemed impenetrable to him, then to her he was an undiscovered country. Even his rages were exotic.

She had met Harry at a party thrown by the English faculty. She had been in her early twenties, and at the end of her course. After that first encounter they had met for coffee, gone to see films together and listened to bands in smoky bars. Harry was funny, always mocking, full of sly jokes about the apparent contradictions of Japan. Under his influence her fellow Japanese began to seem insular and repressed – old fashioned and narrow minded. Now it seemed that those years had been her loss – she had become a foreigner in her own country, an alien to the people around her.

For the first time she had looked at her world, what had seemed normal to her, and was stifled by it. Harry was a breath of fresh air. They had been to Nijo Castle together, to see the palace there. Sachiko had been awed by the huge wooden structure and the intricately painted screens that adorned the walls inside, whilst Harry mocked the signs in English, Chinese and Korean that covered practically every surface. Don't touch the screens. No cameras. No sketches. No stopping. Don't walk on the grass. And after a while even Sachiko, who had grown up with an excess of pedagogical signage, had begun to feel hemmed in by the constant invective.

Now she understood she should have pointed out to Harry that all those signs were there to prevent foreigners from damaging the palace. The rules for Japanese people were unwritten; the habit of respect so ingrained it didn't need to be exhorted. At the time she had been only too ready to repudiate her own people. But the kindness that she had met every day in the refuge centre, after being cut suddenly adrift from her whole life, was causing her to re-evaluate what she had with Harry. Maybe she should have defended her culture from his systematic attack – then perhaps he wouldn't have exerted such a strong control over her during the 10 years that they were together.

In retrospect, Sachiko wondered what had kept Harry in Japan for all these years. He had become increasingly bitter as the decade wore on. He had never suggested that they move to England together. She knew almost nothing about his family. And in the early years that hadn't mattered – they were enough for each other. Once she had become pregnant she started to wonder – about his family, and about the traits that would be inherited by their child. She had the feeling that they were part of the reason why he didn't want to go back. One day, early in the pregnancy, she had broached the subject.

'Harry, do you think we should go and visit your family whilst I can still travel? I won't be allowed to go on a plane when the pregnancy has passed seven months.'

They were eating breakfast, and Harry glared up from the newspaper he'd been reading.

'What? I've told you – I don't have any family in England any more – not that I'd care to announce my impending fatherhood to. What put that idea into your head anyway?'

'Well, it feels a bit different when you're thinking about the next generation. I suppose I'm curious about where you're from. It's strange. It's like I didn't really need to know that before. All we needed was each other. Now I'm curious about the rest. For example, who will his grandparents be? Will he have any cousins?'

'You definitely don't need to think about them now. You know, I told you before – a death in the family shows up people's darker sides. And I asked you not to bring it up again, so I'd rather leave it now if you don't mind.'

Sachiko didn't know what to say, but Harry's attention was already back on his paper, and he didn't seem to need a response. The conversation put him in a bad mood for days, and Sachiko learned to avoid questions about his past.

There was his writing of course. She knew he wanted to write about Japan – but he had always been strangely secretive about it. He said he was working on a book, but that was all. He never discussed it with her – had not even told her whether it was fact or fiction, and would become terrifyingly angry if he thought she was prying. There was one time she really thought he would hit her. It was when she was about seven months pregnant with Tashi, and they had been moving into the new place in Taro. She had been unpacking one of the boxes marked 'Harry, writing'. She had idly picked up a black notebook positioned at the top of the box, the same type he always used, and was scanning through it when she became aware that Harry was standing behind her. He was breathing heavily. She turned around, the black notebook closed, with a finger automatically placed to mark her page.

'What do you think you are doing?'

Sachiko had got a terrible fright but she kept her voice level.

'Unpacking your things, of course.'

His gaze fell to her hands, to the notebook, and his eyes narrowed. He sprang at Sachiko, and snatched it from her suddenly nerveless fingers. She had loved his height, the sheer size of him, but now, with his dark frame towering over her, the rage in his voice, she felt threatened. Automatically she crossed her arms over her belly, sub-consciously protecting the baby inside.

'How dare you nose through my private notebooks. You know I hate you reading that stuff. It's not ready yet.'

'I'm sorry – I was just curious. You never let me see your work.'

'You wouldn't understand it.'

Harry wouldn't meet her eye. He snatched the notebook from her shaking hands and, shoving it on top of all the others, closed the lid of the box firmly, hefting its weight like a feather in the heat of his anger.

'It's private. Here's a tip for you: any boxes with my name on them can stay packed until I decide I'm ready to get to them. I don't want you messing up my things. They're none of your business. Alright?'

His chin thrust out, challenging her, but Sachiko didn't have the energy to pick up this particular gauntlet. She bowed her head obe-diently and left the apartment, with a muttered excuse about greens for dinner. She couldn't remember when he had got so strange and secretive; it was part of everything that had gone wrong.

'What do you feel like eating? It's too hot for noodles. All I want to eat in this weather is tofu and ginger, and a chilled salad!'

Harry shook his head irritably, as if to brush away a fly.

'What did you say?'

'I asked you what you wanted to eat for lunch. It's nearly 12.30pm. Aren't you hungry? You've been staring at that notebook for hours.'

'I've been working for hours you mean. But it's true, I haven't been making much progress. I don't mind – anything's fine – tofu, whatever.'

'Ok – I'll make that then. I've got a pregnancy appointment this afternoon and I'm dreading walking there in this weather.'

'Is there something wrong?'

'No – it's just a routine check. You can come along if you like?'

'Sure, I'll come along. Where is the hospital?'

'It's not at the hospital – it's at the Women's Health Centre. It's not too far – I usually walk there. We can go straight after lunch.'

'Maybe a break will do me good. Anyway – it's about time I got to see the little bugger.'

'Yes – it's lucky the appointment fell in the midterm break this time. And it's always exciting seeing the ultrasound. Dr Yamada thinks he'll be able to tell the sex of the child this time. That is... if you want to know?'

'Of course I want to know! I never understood why people keep it a secret from themselves. Of course it will be a boy, anyway. The firstborns in my family have been boys for generations!'

'So you say,' Sachiko replied dryly, 'but this baby is half Japanese. We shall see! Anyway I'd like to know if the baby is a boy or a girl. It will help me to get to know him or her better. It still feels strange – a whole human life developing inside me! At least if I know if it's a boy or a girl it won't feel like an alien.'

Harry frowned as if he didn't understand her comment. Sachiko busied herself preparing the food, whilst Harry watched her. They ate in silence, and Sachiko washed up and got ready to leave the apartment. They were just about to leave when Sachiko stopped.

'Wait for me a minute. I need to drink another glass of water.'

As usual Harry was impatient. Having made the decision to leave the house he was anxious to be gone.

'I need to pee in a cup when I get there,' Sachiko explained with a blush. 'It's easier to pee if you've had plenty to drink!'

By the time they reached the clinic both of them were sweating. Sachiko pulled out a rabbit-print cloth and used it to mop her forehead and the nape of her neck, before opening the door that led inside.

'I hate Tokyo in August. Now the poor doctor has to deal with a sweaty patient. Still, I suppose they're used to it. Take a seat whilst I let them know we're here.'

Harry watched as Sachiko went over to the desk and gave her name. The clinic didn't seem that busy, and he was the only man. Around him, half a dozen women, mostly alone and in varying stages of pregnancy, flicked through magazines as they waited for their appointments. Sachiko had a brief conversation with the receptionist, and was given a paper cup. She vanished into the restroom and Harry distracted himself by creating stories for the people around him. Sachiko had told him it was normal practice to have an ultrasound scan at every appointment. He didn't know enough about pregnancy to know if that was the same in England. His sister had had a child, and presumably gone through this. Strange he had not so much as thought of his niece in all the years he had been away, and now he was going to be a father, and his child already had a cousin.

Was it always the case, that having a child of your own made you re-evaluate the family ties you thought you had cut? It was an interesting question.

Sachiko came back then, the paper cup discreetly covered with a tissue.

'It shouldn't be too long – the doctor is running on time today.'

'That's good. I was just about to consider trying to distract myself with some of these magazines. I suppose men don't tend to come to these kinds of places that often?'

'Not that often, no. It's still mostly seen as a woman's business. There's no taboo against it, it's just not that common. I guess maybe it's changing slowly.'

'Like everything here!'

He considered sharing his thoughts – about his niece, and how his sister's experience might compare to Sachiko's. But something stopped him; he'd got out of the habit of sharing, and talking about what was going on inside. The upshot was these kind of stilted conversations.

There was a discreet ping, and Sachiko's name came up on the board.

'I'll see you in a minute. It's room two, and the receptionist will let you know when to come in.'

Harry thought it was a bit odd that he had to wait, but that was obviously how it worked here. He sat, fidgeting, until the receptionist signalled to him, then strode towards room number two. A silver plate was embossed with the doctor's name, in kanji and Roman characters. He gave a brief knock and opened the door.

Sachiko was reclined on a chair, chatting cheerfully with the doctor, her stomach bared. A screen to her left was blank at present.

'*Konnichiwa*, Doctor. I'm Harry Turnbull, Sachiko's husband. Pleased to meet you.'

'Good afternoon, Mr Turnbull. Please, take a seat.' The doctor motioned him to an empty chair, and continued in rapid Japanese, which Harry strained to follow. He gathered that Dr Yamada was telling Sachiko about their child's stage of development. On the table was a plastic doll, about the length of a small melon. Sachiko saw him looking and waited for a break in the monologue, before speaking deferentially.

'*Gomenasai*, Doctor-san. May I explain to my husband?'

'Of course!' The doctor paused.

Sachiko turned to Harry.

'Dr Yamada was just explaining how big the baby is now – about the same size as that model on the table. Can you believe our baby has grown so much already?'

'It is amazing,' replied Harry in English. 'I didn't realise that babies were so fully formed at only five months – it's a small human! That's amazing! *Sugoi, na?*'

Dr Yamada smiled, and started speaking again, a little more slowly this time, whilst applying a clear gel to Sachiko's exposed stomach. He started to run the ultrasound wand round the softly rising slope of her belly and suddenly they both saw the screen come to life. Harry had seen pictures of ultrasound scans before, but they never showed detail like this. He had assumed it would be the usual grainy 2D scan, but this had depth and was astonishingly detailed. 'It really is amazing!' He found himself saying again, and reached over to clasp Sachiko's hand. He looked to see if he could see any genitals, and there it was.

'So, you didn't think we'd be having a boy, Sachiko? That looks like a fine boy to me! Dr Yamada – does that look like a boy to you?'

'It does indeed. I'm just going to take some measurements to ensure that his development is just where it should be for this stage, but it all looks good to me. Would you like a picture to take away with you?'

'Yes please, Dr Yamada.'

Sachiko sat up and adjusted her clothing. She hadn't commented on the gender of their child, and Harry wondered if she was secretly disappointed. He didn't care. He squeezed her hand again and smiled at her. Sachiko looked back at him, with an unreadable expression, before turning her attention again to Dr Yamada. He was busy at his computer, recording the details of the session, and with a final flourish at the keys turned back to them. 'Well, Mr and Mrs Turnbull, it seems all is proceeding as expected, and you can look forward to a healthy baby boy if all continues to go smoothly. I'll see you at your next check-up.'

'Thank you very much, Dr Yamada.' Sachiko bowed as she spoke, and Harry somewhat clumsily followed. They went back out to the reception and Harry waited whilst Sachiko took her records to the receptionist to be updated and collected the picture. There were fewer women now in the waiting room, and Harry found himself looking at them with slightly different eyes. They were not just pregnant females, but prospective parents, like Sachiko and himself. They weren't just bumps, and swollen ankles, and strange aches and pains – but growing and developing babies. Sachiko finished up and came over to him, and he felt a sudden protective urge that made him reach out to take her arm as he ushered her through the door.

'Thanks! So how was that for you?'

'It was great! Don't you feel the same way? It's incredible to see our son growing inside you!'

'Sure, I'm very happy that the baby's healthy and doing well. But it wasn't the first time for me. The ultrasound is astonishing before you get used to it.'

'And we're having a boy – I hate to say I told you so but...'

'Yes, you were right. A little boy. Our son! I'm not sure what to think about it yet – I'm just happy that it's a human and doing so well.'

'It's not an it – "it" is a he!'

'You're right – he's doing so well. It's a lot to get used to. At least we know now.'

Sachiko fell silent, and looking across Harry could see that she was looking pensive.

'What's wrong, Sachiko?'

'I was wondering if I should tell my parents about the child. I haven't been in contact with them for a while. It doesn't feel right not to tell them about their first grandchild though. I'm not sure what to do.'

'I can't tell you what to do. I was thinking about my family too, earlier – about when my sister was pregnant with my niece. It's not like we're planning on running over there immediately. Let's wait and see what happens, shall we?'

'You're probably right. It's been a long time since we were in touch, and what if something went wrong? It's better to wait a while. Oh, it's too hot to think! Let's just get home and we can talk about it when we get there.'

They walked back slowly. If anything, it had got even hotter and muggier during the brief hour they had spent at the clinic. Both were silent, each of them thinking, considering, marvelling over the new life they had seen developing on the scanner. For Sachiko it was the latest of several snapshots, each documenting and charting the life growing inside her. But a boy! She tried to imagine what he would be like. Would he grow up to tower over her, like Harry? Reflexively, she stroked her belly. In the last week there had been a distinct 'pop' and she had gone from possibly chubby to definitely pregnant. Her navel now pointed out. It was a strange and unsettling sensation; her whole centre of balance had changed. She felt a moment of panic as the inevitability of it all overwhelmed her – the birth and bringing this new person into the world; and then a calm feeling overtook her as they waited to cross a busy road, and a small child, hand clasped tight in his mother's, gazed up at her with trusting eyes. A part of her mind wryly blamed endorphins, but it felt good, all the same, to welcome this new person into their life. As the lights changed and the tide of humans swept forward she felt Harry's guiding hand in the small of her back, and turned to look at him fleetingly. He was lost in abstraction, his action automatic.

For Harry, the clinic visit and the ultrasound had been a lot to take in. Up till now he had taken a backseat in the pregnancy – content to receive regular reports from Sachiko, but not really connected to the whole process. Suddenly, viscerally, he felt his son. His child's heartbeat, heard through the sonogram, echoed through his head and set up a sympathetic rhythm in his chest. His child! His son! He started listing in his head all those things he imagined a father would share with his son, but immediately he came up against the strangeness of being in Japan. Football was big here, but Harry had never been into sports. Walking, the wilderness – that was the thing. And who knew where they would be by the time their son was old enough to be walking? He looked over at Sachiko again, noticing afresh how her gait had changed in this new stage of pregnancy. It would be a while before they breathed the fresh mountain air of the National Park again together. What with the winter, and now her developing pregnancy, they had not left Tokyo together for months. Well, the move up north would help with that – it would all be on their doorstep.

九

It hurts to breathe. I hope I'm not developing a chest infection. It's getting colder – I can't get warm.

I'm not sure if I'm going insane. Maybe if I write it down it will make more sense. I was out gathering firewood for the stove in the cabin when my foot snagged on a root, and I nearly landed on my face. I lay there, eyes closed for a moment, recovering from the impact, and when I opened them again there was Tashi.

He was older, but I recognised him – he was a mix of Sachiko and myself, but he had changed. He had the size, but not the appearance, of a three-month-old baby, and, although he was undeniably present, he wasn't quite 'there' – his feet not quite making contact with the ground, and a slight shimmer about him that suggested a creature less than solid. His face was sunken, somehow mummified, his limbs and torso narrow, making his distended belly seem even more enormous, his frail head balanced upon a long, thin neck. Tashi couldn't be there. Could he?

Then he spoke for the first time.

'Hey, Papa – bet you didn't expect to see me again so soon did you? Sorry to break in on your idyll, but I think we have some unfinished business?'

I felt the world whirling around me, my vision blurred, sounds muffled as though my ears were stopped with cotton; my heart beating with irregular thumps against the cage of my chest. I felt like I was coming apart at the joints. I didn't trust myself to stand, or speak. I closed my eyes and willed the apparition to disappear. If I just lay there for a few moments, maybe the hallucination would go away.

Gradually the muffled feeling in my ears cleared, and I could hear the sounds of birdsong and the breeze murmuring. I kept my eyes closed and lay where I had fallen, feeling the damp ground beneath my fingertips. I willed myself to become calm, and focussed on the sounds around me.

'What, silence? And your only beloved son come back to keep you company on your journey? You were just wondering what you'll need for the wilderness... yes I can read your thoughts too. Don't worry though – I won't tell anyone else how dark they are.'

That voice again – a curious high lisp with a vicious edge. I opened my eyes and looked up, raising myself to my elbows as I did so. There was the strange wizened homunculus that was still, recognisably, my son. There were his eyes, which still hadn't darkened from the blue he had been born with, the cowlick he had inherited from me, and the bow-shaped lips that Sachiko had given him. Now they were twisted in a mocking grin.

I couldn't speak. I knew I had to get away. I pulled myself to my feet, all without being able to drag my eyes away from him. I seemed drawn into those milky pools.

I turned my back and focussed on getting myself under control. It had to be a hallucination. I gave myself a vicious pinch on the upper arm, which hurt like buggery but it was no good. The voice came again.

'Don't ignore me, Papa. We've got a lot to talk about you and I.'

If I couldn't make it go away, then maybe I could outrun it. I turned back so that I was facing the path. The figure was still there, blocking my way and grinning sardonically at me. I closed my eyes again and sprinted through it – arms held before me as though I was breaking the ribbon at the end of a race. I heard laughter behind me over the thudding of my steps. I kept running for a long time.

+

Time passes. Children are not allowed to play in the streets. Schools hand out dosimeters, to measure radiation. There is a general feeling of not enough information, of life on hold, of boredom. The main industry in Kuji is fishing, but most of the boats were destroyed by the tsunami, and, although more have been donated by Hakodate City, refrigeration plants take longer to rebuild. Here and there are impromptu shrines with flowers and small stuffed toys. Neat piles of rubble sit on the edges of land stripped bare. Elsewhere, all seems normal: car parks by the sea wall still filled with neatly lined-up vehicles – as though the sea had never swept over those suddenly puny defences to eat up everything in its hungry maw.

The fate of the nuclear reactors at Fukushima, in danger of meltdown after multiple breaches of their cooling chambers, is at the forefront of everyone's mind. There is a sense of apocalypse, of the world ending, of everything changing into something else. All over the North, villages, towns and cities are being evacuated, displacing hundreds of thousands of people; all the tiny rituals of daily life shattered.

Round-faced Americans and Europeans arrive to help with the relief efforts. Messages of support pour in from around the world, but little changes. The refuge centre gradually empties. Those who cannot afford better are moved to flimsy temporary accommodation, which gives the illusion of privacy – although the walls are so thin each sound carries, and the lack of insulation makes every night a battle against the cold. Within each enclosure, tattered futons hold those survivors that remain from each family, and from them come hushed sounds of life, their smothered grief. The knowledge of what has happened begins to settle, and becomes the new normal. People start to make plans for what happens next.

The government provides relief funds, but they are barely enough to buy food with – and won't stretch to clothes to replace those left behind in the mad flight for safety. Tons of supplies come in from other parts of Japan, but there is little coordination and much of it remains unopened – the gifts mute testimony to blind generosity.

Kuji school gymnasium is packed with crates, which vie for space with heaps of recovered belongings, now starting to be sorted into neat piles. Every day more come in, and anyone up for volunteering is welcome to help classify and box it up.

In between checking for news, Sachiko and Hiroko helped with the sorting. They had grown closer in the weeks since the tsunami. Hiroko had been reunited with her son, but there was still no sign of her husband, and now she, the child and her mother were waiting to be rehoused. Until then they were stuck in the no-man's-land of temporary accommodation. With time on their hands, they had got to know each other, and Sachiko had found herself able to open up more than was usual with her.

Hiroko held up a pair of enormous French-style lace panties.

'Do we have a bin named "seduction underwear"?'

Sachiko sat back on her hands and looked at Hiroko. From the roof lights a shaft of sunlight slanted down and misted her hair. Soft strands escaped from the neat twist Hiroko had pinned her hair up in, her face glowed and her eyes sparkled. Sachiko wondered how Hiroko could be so merry, with her husband still amongst the missing – but she was naturally irrepressible.

'I don't imagine the owner of those pants will be claiming them back soon. She'd be too embarrassed!' she replied.

'You're right at that. Can you imagine? What if it's a man?'

At that Sachiko couldn't resist a smile – the image was so ridiculous.

'Sumo wrestler on his night off.'

Hiroko giggled.

'I wonder if he's got suspenders to go with it?'

'Well, it's not that likely in Kuji after all – maybe in Roppongi. I hear anything goes there!'

They continued sorting companionably. It was bright and quiet in the hall, and the spring sunlight warmed the air and sent dust motes dancing. Sachiko's mind was focussed on the task in front of her. So many photographs! Strange – it had never occurred to her to take the family photographs from the *Butsudan*, but there had been no sign of them anyway in the mud-strewn matchsticks that were all that remained of their home. Look at this one – a stern man of the older Japanese type stared out of a dark background. She couldn't stay here forever. Sooner or later she was going to have to accept that she wasn't going to find them here. Fewer bodies were being recovered each day. Almost none from the sea. Surely if they had left, if they had escaped, Harry would have found a way to contact her? But he probably thought she was dead. There was nothing left of their apartment block and in fact it was a miracle she had survived at all. Information was patchy, and his Japanese had never been good – there was no guarantee he could even find the refugee lists for this town.

Sachiko wanted to ask Hiroko about how she felt about her husband's disappearance, but didn't know how to frame the question. She should have been able to ask – after all, they were in the same predicament; but she couldn't bear to wipe the joyful sparkle from those eyes. She wondered what their relationship was like. Hiroko was so much more open, less self-conscious than herself.

Hiroko was quick to sense Sachiko's change of mood, or she wasn't as good at hiding her feelings as she thought.

'What are you thinking, Sachiko? You can tell me – don't be shy.'

Sachiko's words came out in a rush and she blushed furiously.

'Hiroko, do you think you'll see your husband again?'

Hiroko was quiet for a little while. She looked down at her hands. Then she started to speak in a low and steady voice.

'I know he'll turn up. I feel like I would know if he was dead. He's not a man of many words, but we've always had a connection, you know?'

'I think so. I think I had that with Harry once.'

'The men have always left. It's the fishing. They go to sea, and sometimes they don't come back. You learn to feel the difference. It doesn't feel like that.'

They both fell silent and continued with their work. The silence had a different quality now, each in their own world.

And what should she do now? Taro had attracted them because they had no ties there – but this was the very reason it held nothing for her now. It was a small community, and had pulled even closer together since the disaster. There was little time, or love, for strangers. Kuji, the nearest town of any size to Taro, had welcomed the refugees, but she felt little connection to the place, although she had to admire the determination of people intent on building 'a brand new city' to replace what had been destroyed.

It was time to move on. Despite her fears about where she could move to, and what she could do there, it was obvious there was nothing for her in Aomori prefecture any more. Kuji had been a refuge for a little while, but there was no reason for her to stay in the North East. The meagre government compensation, plus her small savings, should tide her over until she could find a job in Tokyo, or maybe further south, in Osaka. The one person she would miss was Hiroko – it had been far too long since she had had a friend.

Maybe that's where she had got the habit of not sharing? So much left unsaid – even though she felt as close to Hiroko as to anyone else.

She had that closeness once with Harry, but they had lost it after Tashi was born. And she wondered if in fact there had ever been true closeness with another person – even Tashi, her own son. She realised that she had spent her life constructing places to hide her feelings and ambitions. Her mental room had become a very real prison after Tashi was born, but it had always been there, waiting to become fact.

As if reading her thoughts, Hiroko asked suddenly, 'What will you do next, Sachiko?'

'I honestly don't know, Hiroko. We came here to get away from everything – so that Harry could write – so that I could bring up our son. But there's not much here for me now.'

'Will you go to your family? They're in the South aren't they?'

'Yes – Osaka. I don't think they were much affected by the earthquake. But I haven't even told them I'm alive.'

Hiroko's eyes widened in shock, 'Really? But why not? You need family now, at a time like this, surely? They must be frantic.'

'We've been out of touch for a long time. Ever since I married Harry. They don't even know I moved to Taro. They probably assume I'm still living in Tokyo. I'd rather not talk about it right now, if you don't mind.'

Hiroko was silent. Sachiko knew that Hiroko could never understand why she felt this way – but that she would not dream of criticising. Although their situations seemed so similar, there would always be a distance between them.

'Do you think it's safe to go outside?' Hiroko wondered. 'I heard they're giving the school kids some kind of glass badge – to measure the radiation levels. It doesn't feel like it's safe. What do you think, Sachiko?'

'I think they're not telling us everything. And who knows what effect the wind and the rain will have? It's like a silent death. But then is anywhere safe? They're saying the radiation has drifted all the way to America.'

'It's so hard! But we'll get through it. We have to.' Hiroko's face was determined. 'We've been here before.'

Sachiko knew she was right. They would work together and they would get through it – like Hiroshima, like the thousand tremblings of the earth that left buildings mutilated and families scattered. Yes. They would get through it and build again; but at what cost?

She stood up and went to fetch another box to sort – this one full of clothes and shoes. It was an incongruous selection. Would they ever be paired? What were the odds that the matching shoes survived, and made it to this centre? She knew they would never rest until everything was rebuilt.

As she came back with the box, Hiroko looked up, smiling. 'Look at what I found!'

It was an oversized, and rather knobbly, pink dildo.

Sachiko grinned back. 'Another one for the seduction pile I think. Maybe we should open our own sex shop! And what about you? What are your plans?'

Hiroko's family had lived in Taro for generations, but over the years all had moved away until only her immediate family were left. Her father had gone missing during the tsunami, and now all that remained were her mother and son.

'We'll stay in temporary accommodation until we can find somewhere new to live I think. But there's no guarantee that will ever be in Taro. Ours is a small family – I have an uncle in the South, but he's very old. We'll probably end up in the city. I'll have to get a job!'

Hiroko looked so surprised at the thought that Sachiko found herself chuckling. 'What will you do?'

'I don't know. Work in a shop? Answer the phone?'

'Have you always worked in the family shop?'

'Yes – I've never had a real job, or had to deal with any bills or taxes – all of that stuff is so complicated! I married young and had Taiki almost immediately. Anyway, I'm sure I'll find something. I've got health and youth on my side! Maybe I could be a paid companion to some old person who lost their family.'

'That's an idea. You'd be great at cheering up someone like that... but how would that work with your little boy?'

'Well, he'll be at school soon, so I'll have all day to fill. And of course my mother can help with looking after him. Anyway – he'll just have to get used to it. Life just won't be the same for us any more. Or for anyone.'

I don't know how long I have been here. Something strange is going on with my memory and my sense of time. I am filthy and covered in scratches. I'm not sure where I am. The burn in my muscles is that sharp second-day pain that tells of sinew pushed to the limit and then further. I stretch painfully while trying to get a sense of my location and the time of day. The sun is over the zenith – it must be afternoon. I can't tell how much time I've lost. Nothing is familiar.

It's a very different landscape here. I can tell I'm much higher up, deeper into the mountains. Perhaps I'm not even in the National Park any more, but have crossed into the restricted zone. I don't want to be here, come nightfall, without any shelter or food. I pat myself down, make a quick inventory of what I have on me. My knife is still there, thank goodness.

My mind flits to Tashi; I had a sense he'd been there all along with me on that heedless flight, goading me. But how could he be here? Maybe I am psychotic. I've never believed in ghosts.

It's not a question I can answer now, and I can't see any sign of him. I decide to head downhill and see if I can pick up a marker for one of the hiking trails that meander around the foothills.

With no path to guide me the going is tough, and I spend most of my time scrambling up and down rocky slopes, grabbing at young conifers to keep my balance. Soon my hands are raw and sticky with resin, and my shoulders ache.

Suddenly Tashi is there again, right ahead of me. Once again, he doesn't seem quite substantial – it's as if I could see right through him if I squinted hard enough, and he shimmers slightly, like a thermal on a hot day. Every detail of his appearance is identical to the first time. If I'm hallucinating, my mind is remarkably consistent.

'Hi, Papa. Did you miss me?'

That reedy voice. Of course, I never heard the real Tashi speak. My son is still too young for anything but screaming, and, rarely, gurgling. This Tashi speaks perfect English, again with that sardonic lilt to his voice.

'Of course you did, you must have been lonely in the forest for all these days. And you're not looking so hot either. Don't worry, I'm going to stick around this time.'

I don't reply. I look at him, silently, my hands resting at my sides, but ready for flight. The sheer terror that I felt the first time I saw him is absent now. And maybe it makes sense that he's here. I should have realised I couldn't get away so easily, no matter how much I might want to leave them behind.

'What a dreadful thing to think, Papa. Guilty conscience? But no, you wouldn't feel guilt. True psychotics never do.'

I say nothing, turn my back and keep walking. Maybe he'll get bored. I'm determined to find my way back to the cabin. As I walk I can hear him singing, tunelessly, behind me.

'Rock-a-bye baby in the tree top, rock-a-bye baby in the tree top. When the wind blows, the cradle will fall, and down will fall baby, and cradle, and all.'

I had sung him that nursery rhyme over and over, a useless mantra against his determined sleeplessness. As I walked I heard him singing, again and again. I tried to tune it out and concentrate on finding my way.

The singing gets closer and then I can feel a cold and insubstantial weight settling on my shoulders. Strangely when he speaks I can feel his breath against my ear.

'Papa – I'm curious – just what is your plan? You can't just escape into the wilderness like some modern-day Heathcliff...'

I try to ignore him. I can't spare breath just now to answer the boy – a figment, surely? Only a projection of my subconscious would refer to *Wuthering Heights*, here in the wilderness of Japan.

'Are you listening, Papa? What are you looking for out here? I don't think you'll find it. I think you'll die out here and no one will ever find your bones.'

Above his voice, the call of a bird – a wild sound, piercing and free. An eagle? Looking up, I see it circling – searching for prey, or waiting for the moment to pounce.

'Aw – you're no fun, Papa – they told me you wouldn't be but I wouldn't believe them. It's even more boring there though. All those spirits, stuck in limbo until the 49th day. And no one to burn even a little incense for me. It's such a comfort when you're on the spirit plane. But what would you know? You're an atheist! Guess you feel a little silly now, huh?'

I feel hemmed in, trapped in a way I never thought possible in this wild place. Why is he torturing me, this manifestation, or hallucination, or whatever the damned thing is? Where has he taken me? I don't know whether I'm more worried about being lost in the wilderness, or tormented by this sarcastic apparition. At least if he went away I could concentrate on trying to find my way back to the cabin. My thoughts feel scattered when he's around, like he's projecting some kind of field.

'That would be nice, wouldn't it, Papa? Sorry that's not how it works. I'm just going to keep riding your back until you set me free.'

With that he falls silent, but I can still feel his cold fingers on my neck. What did he mean? Is there something that I'm missing? I feel a moment of vertigo, like I'm trying to visualise the size of the universe. Nothing has felt quite right for many days now. I thought by leaving, by surviving this wilderness and becoming at home in it, I was coming back to myself. I feel sane. Yet there is the problem of Tashi, which seems insoluble. Got to find my way back to the cabin, then I can start to make sense of it. Don't talk to him. Don't let him know that you know he's there. But that's damn hard when the ghost, or manifestation, or whatever it is, seems to be able to read my thoughts. Changeling? Something about him reminds me of the faerie myths of old, the Sidhe that kidnapped children and replaced them with their own, beings with strange powers. They said you could always tell by the eyes – they had a peculiar light in them.

And then of course there were the many ghost stories of Japan, which always seemed to be set in the mountains. I had come across a lot of them researching my book. It was said that they often haunted murderers, but I don't think I ever murdered anyone. Least of all my son.

Sachiko keeps busy, losing herself in daily tasks, falling into a rhythm. There is the cooking, childcare; the constant labour of sorting, and cleaning, and mending; the endless laundry. The days pass. Life goes on. She tries not to think – but she can't help remembering, analysing, daydreaming with vivid flashes of memory. In the absence of the real Harry, she starts to remember the man she had first met. Those early days, when their love was fresh and new.

The memories come slowly – it's as if that part of their relationship had been totally eclipsed by Tashi. She can barely recall anything of the weeks leading up to the tsunami, but the memory of her first meeting with Harry is perfectly clear.

'Hello – *do you mind if I join you?*'

Three or four of them had been chatting about the course when the tall dark-haired English man approached them. Sachiko hadn't seen him around the campus before. He was the kind of person you tended to notice, because, as well as his height, he had an imposing presence. Sachiko felt a poke in the ribs and realised she'd suddenly been cast in the role of spokesperson.

'Of course not – *nice to meet you. This is Natsuko, Ruri and Umeko, and my name is Sachiko.*'

The quick switch to English meant that this came out a bit more stilted than she would have liked. Despite her degree, she was still more comfortable with the written language.

'Well, it's very nice to meet you all, and a beautiful day to be in the park. Thank goodness Tokyo has some nice green spaces like this to escape from the madness.'

'Are you visiting, or do you live here?'

'I'm planning on living here. I'm teaching English at the moment. I've been here for two months already.'

'And how are you finding it?'

'The teaching part is easy. "How to Japan" is a little harder. I think I need a guide.'

Was he flirting with her? Sachiko hadn't met that many foreigners, apart from her lecturers, and they were all ancient. And, confusingly, she felt an instant attraction to him. She had been on dates of course – everyone did that – but they never got past a peck on the cheek. So she was shocked to feel an actual animal rush of blood inside that brought a corresponding blush to her cheeks.

Later he told her that he had been struck by her the moment he had seen her, and that was why he'd introduced himself. By then she had already fallen in love.

She knew it must be love because everything felt so different. Sachiko had to admit that, up until she had met Harry, she had lived life at one remove. She wasn't unhappy, but she couldn't quite get that worked up about anything either. Life happened; one thing came after the next, and so she came to be at a party thrown by the English faculty in nearby Komaba Park. And there she met Harry.

They had left the party, and wandered to the nearby folk museum, where there was a beautiful traditional stile in the middle of a formal garden. It was a peaceful place to sit and get to know each other better. Almost before they knew it closing time had arrived. Sachiko had never met anyone like Harry before – it was as if a new world were opening up to her with every moment that they spent together. Her initial shyness at being seen with a foreigner soon vanished, as the afternoon darkened into evening, and Harry invited her to eat with him. They went to a little place she knew near Ueno Park – only 16 seats, with mellow jazz coming from the stereo, and one guy behind the counter balletically creating a constant stream of delicacies for his customers. It was all new and delightful for Harry.

He had asked her to show him Japan, so they did lots of tourist stuff together on the weekends – wandering around the Imperial Palace; peddling around Kyoto, exploring its many temples together. Harry loved the mamacharis, *the ever-adaptable Japanese workhorse bicycles, although he struggled to find one big enough to accommodate his long legs. They found a small temple with hundreds of small sculptures carved out of blocks of cement – diminutive mossy Buddhas that looked ancient, until you noticed anachronistic details: here was one holding a camera; there was one with a phone, and a playful expression on his face; another was giving the universal signal of peace.*

Hiroko broke into her train of thought.

'What do you miss most about your old life, Sachiko?'

Sachiko dragged herself out of her reverie with a start.

'Hmm? Sorry, Hiroko – I was far away. What did you say?'

The two of them were folding laundry, a seemingly never-ending task. With so many children amongst the survivors, there was always a shortage of clean clothes and bedding. The only way they could keep ahead was by setting aside time every day to reduce the backlog. Sachiko didn't mind. Hiroko had been right about keeping busy.

'Well, maybe it was a foolish question. I asked, "What do you miss most about your old life?" – but perhaps it's best not to dwell on before.'

'It's ok – I was just thinking about it actually. I was remembering when I first met Harry. I don't know if he's what I miss most though. I miss Tashi. It's strange – it feels like I've learned more about him since he's been missing, and about love. I was so absent before that I didn't really get to experience him as a mother – I spent my whole time avoiding everyone, and hiding myself away. I never learned to love him.'

Hiroko was quiet when Sachiko finished, and she immediately regretted her openness. What would Hiroko think about a woman who didn't seem to care about her husband, or love her son?

But Hiroko was merely thinking.

'It must be even harder for you, Sachiko – because it seems like you're not sure how to feel about the ones who were lost. You can't mourn, because their bodies haven't been found. You can't let go, because you didn't say goodbye. It's like they've become ghosts – like they can't rest until their stories are finished. Who knows, there could be ghosts all around us. All those thousands of people, lost in an instant, and no one to say the sutras, to honour their spirits, and set them free.'

Sachiko considered this.

'You're probably right. Every time I try to remember Harry, it's something negative. That's why I was thinking about when we first met. It was a beautiful time. I suppose that's something I miss, but I'm not sure that counts, because it's been so long since it was like that. But, Hiroko – you loved your husband. It must be very different for you.'

Hiroko didn't reply immediately, and when she did her voice trembled.

'I don't know, Sachiko. It seems everything has broken into a million pieces – like a shattered mirror. All the things that were connected are now so many brittle shards, reflecting craziness. You don't know what to do next. So you just do something… anything to fill the gap. We were all living our lives, living our stories. And then it was all gone – like someone took a giant laser and stripped our home of trees, and houses, and people, and everything that had once been knitted together. I don't know where we are. I don't know where we need to go next. I don't even know what will happen tomorrow.'

Sachiko leaned over and gave her a hug. They held each other wordlessly for a little while, and then Sachiko leaned back and looked Hiroko in the eyes.

'You'll go on. I know you can, Hiroko.'

'Well, I'm trying to remember the happy times – it's the only thing that drives away the numbness. Everyone has lost someone – some have lost everyone. It feels selfish to complain. I suppose what I miss is the feeling of cosiness, of completeness, of home. Of *uchi*. Eating together as a family. Of course there were stresses, but it felt like everything was in balance. I want to make that balance again for my son. I want to restore our *uchi*.'

Sachiko considered this, and realised that wasn't what she wanted. She wanted to get away. She tried to put it into words.

'For me… I just want to leave it all behind and start again. That's the only way I'll be able to move on. The only way I can accept what's happened and be free.'

'So when will you go?'

Sachiko's answer came quickly, and her tone was determined.

'As soon as I can. I'll go to Tokyo, and find a room, and get a job, and start again. I've got to do it, Hiroko.'

They looked at each other across a gulf, as if the miles had already opened up between them.

'I'll miss you, Sachiko.'

'I'll miss you too, Hiroko – but we can keep in touch.'

They fell silent again, and lost themselves in the piles of laundry.

十三

Night is nearly here again – sunset a brief glory of red and gold skies that soon fades into darkness. I've been walking all day, and the landscape has been gradually changing – massive ancient cedars of the higher reaches replaced by the endless conifers of the foothills, but I still haven't found so much as a marker to suggest where I am. The forest is very quiet – barely the call of a bird disturbs the peace, and even the rustle of leaves is muted. It's as if other forms of life have given up the struggle to compete with these recent imports – no fungus, not so much as a bracket, fringes their trunks, and the forest floor is carpeted with pine needles that dull my steps.

'News update!'

Tashi sounds gleeful. 'The situation at Fukushima is worsening. They have no control over two of the cores. Who knows how much radiation is escaping out to sea from the leaking coolant water? The government isn't saying anyway. Allegedly it's perfectly safe and there's no danger. Ha! Let's change the channel. That's funny – it's on all the channels! Well, Papa – there's a turn-up for the books. Looks like we'll all be radioactive soon. This just in from *The Asahi Shimbun*: "The megathrust tsunami event has caused a developing situation at the Fukushima nuclear plant, and has left some of the fuel rods exposed, raising the risk of the reactor overheating and melting down. The army has been trying to cool the rods with seawater to stop the reactor going into meltdown." Poor little fishies, eh, Pops?'

I don't know what to make of this. His voice has switched to that of a news presenter. I can see his lips moving, but the sound is coming out crackly and full of static. It's as if he's channelling a radio station. If this is a dream it's a pretty damn convincing one. And if it's not, and the power station at Fukushima really has been damaged by the tsunami, the consequences will be devastating for Japan. Not only is Fukushima a large city itself, but it is terrifyingly close to Tokyo. I try to imagine the scale of the damage, and fail. If Fukushima was affected, the whole north-east coast must have got it.

'Papa – you're obviously not listening to me. Here is Japan – threatened more than it has ever been before. And you say you're a writer? You've been sitting in your pathetic hovel for all these weeks scribbling, and not a word about your family, about the tsunami, about all those deaths. It's as if you don't even care.'

This was too much. My lips started moving almost before my brain had processed the instruction.

'And what have I achieved? Nothing. I can't write any more. From the moment you were conceived, my muse died.'

'Your muse? No wonder you can't write a word when you spout crap like that, dear Father. Write about what you know: that's where it's at, Papa.'

'Oh, what do you know? Another news bulletin from our great and esteemed leaders. They've been using police water cannons, fire trucks and military helicopters to douse the core with bucket after bucket of water. Doesn't seem to be working out too well for them though – what a shame. The UN Nuclear Agency isn't happy about the situation at all. What do you think will happen if it all gets worse, Papa? There's still another reactor to go.'

'Oh yes, it's all kicking off down there. What next for this shitty world eh? I don't like it any more than you. What did I ever have? Three months of life with two crazy parents. And now dragged back to this.'

I look straight at Tashi. His wizened features have lost their merry cast and he looks merely old and sad. It's damn spooky – like looking at an older version of myself. I can't hold his gaze, so I look away. When I glance back Tashi is gone.

Could he really be just a projection of my mind? Here, and not here, channelling the news like some kind of ghostly radio receiver? Even if he is part of my subconscious mind, how could he know things I'm not consciously aware of? I'm going crazy.

It's getting colder; night will be here soon. In this light the landscape has an uncanny aspect – I feel the terror of the sublime. For just a moment I am thrown into confusion; a vertigo-inducing welter of alternate interpretations; a strange universe populated by changelings and vengeful ghosts. Tilt shift. I feel my feet on the ground, the whisper of the breeze on my cheek. I keep walking.

As I suspected, once I reach low ground, I run into a hiker's trail – one of the many walks that meander around the edges of the National Park. I'm even starting to recognise some landmarks now that I've reached the foothills, which means I'm not so far from my little cabin. The going underfoot is easy, downhill, which is lucky, as I don't think I've eaten anything since before I first saw Tashi and fled headlong into the forest, which must have been several days ago. I'm feeling lightheaded, but, still, it's good to breathe crisp air. Well-worn roots and hand-smoothed branches positioned conveniently at steep places make the path easy to navigate, leaving my mind free to think.

It has been getting steadily colder – just keeping warm is a constant battle. All it would take was a broken leg, and I could easily die out here in the wilderness. Even in normal times few people pass this way. The chances of someone finding me now, with the whole country apparently in crisis mode, are vanishingly slim.

'Scared are you, Papa? I told you you'd be food for birds soon enough, but you wouldn't listen, would you?'

Tashi often appears during my moments of self-doubt – as though his greatest pleasure is to torture me.

'You're right, Papa – that is one of the few compensations left to me. Not that you care but I thought a little news bulletin might break the monotony. Radiation levels in Tokyo? Power cuts in Nagoya? The deepening recession? We're really spoiled for choice it seems. The contamination is spreading ALL over Japan – apparently Tokyo tap water is not safe for infants now! Must be REALLY bad for the government to admit something like that. Lucky I'm dead and the radiation can't harm me eh? I wonder what long-term effect all this radioactive iodine will have on a generation growing up in a nuclear reality?'

'There must be some good news!' I didn't want to acknowledge Tashi's attempts to goad me, but I was learning that ignoring Tashi did little good. He would go on anyway – and I was beginning to forget the sound of my own voice – I had to talk to someone soon or

I would start to go mad. I found myself laughing, in short bitter barks that I struggled to control.

Tashi's laugh echoed my own. 'Start to go mad? You're already as mad as a hatter, dear Father.' Maybe he's the voice of my subconscious. What am I doing here in the wilderness listening to a ghost decide which news report to torture me with next? 'You're getting to look quite the part of the wild woodsman, Papa – guess packing a razor or a mirror wasn't high on your list of priorities when you did a runner. I'm glad I can't smell – you must be pretty high by now. So, where was I – ah, here we are…'

'According to the *Asahi Shimbun,* radioactive iodine levels in seawater near the stricken Fukushima nuclear plant have reached a new record! Four thousand three hundred and eighty-five times the legal limit. That doesn't look like changing any time soon. They're still trying to stop the cores melting down. Maybe you're smarter than you look. I wouldn't want to be too close to Fukushima right now.'

Of course I pretended that I couldn't hear him. Japan is a densely populated archipelago. I wondered how many people had been affected by the quake.

What about Sachiko? I've been avoiding thinking about her up till now. She must think I'm dead. I've been missing for weeks now. It feels like I've closed that chapter of my life. Tashi seems to know things that he shouldn't, but he hasn't given me a clue whether she's alive or dead. I wonder how many survived in our street? It was right behind the fishing port. The waves must have hit our block. Could Sachiko have survived? I heard the tsunami sirens, even from the outskirts of the town. I'm sure she was unconscious when I left. Surely she hadn't got out in time?

Tashi was quick to answer. I can't get used to the idea that he can read my mind.

'Of course you'd want to know that, Papa. Did you know we're on the list of missing? My poor mother is still holding out hope we'll be found alive. If only she knew… how does that make you feel? Are you even capable of feeling anything at all?'

I didn't answer. There wasn't much to say, and I was saving my breath for the trail ahead. This part of the path was familiar – the cabin should be just ahead. I longed for the feel of four walls about me.

Even if she is alive, I feel like a widower. How would things have been different if I'd somehow roused Sachiko and we both ran the hell out of there? Would she have come? Or would we have perished there together?

'Wouldn't you like to know, Papa? Well, you forfeited that information when you decided to turn your back on Taro. All those brave reserve fire corps volunteers, looking for survivors in the wreckage. Those first 24 hours were crucial you know. You could have saved lives, but instead you ran away. Does that make me a coward too, if I'm descended from one?'

His cold but insubstantial fingers clung to the nape of my neck; his voice a sibilant whispering in my ear. 'What happened to Mama-chan? Where is she now? What would you give me to tell you, Papa?'

The way suddenly grew steep, and I had to use both hands to lower myself down through rocks and past fallen trees. I didn't reply – I was thinking back to the time we'd spent together, but it already felt as though it had happened years ago; I couldn't fit my mind inside the feeling of being with her. When did we fall out of love? Should I be feeling this way? Even if she is alive, I have no desire to find her. I left that life behind.

Again the cold touch at my neck, the reminder, that reedy voice, 'What makes you think you can leave any of it behind?'

I turned a corner and, blessedly, the cabin was there in front of me. I hadn't latched the door when I left, and it swung on its hinges, but it didn't look like anyone had been there in my absence. It felt good to be back in my refuge, after the days of wandering. I felt as though I had come home.

I went to bed and slept well and the next morning dawned bright and with more than a promise of spring. There had been no sign of Tashi and I began to feel more secure; maybe it had just been a hallucination brought on by hunger, and fear.

Everything will be better now, and this nightmare of Tashi will end.

Once she had made the decision to leave, everything seemed to happen very quickly. It was a contrast to the months she had spent preparing their move to Tohoku in the first place. A few phone calls, a vague plan, and the next day she was on her way out of there. An accommodation agency had sent her a list of apartments to rent in various areas of Tokyo, and she had already arranged to view one of them, filled with a desire to be moving, to give herself a destination. She packed her few possessions quickly, ready for the lengthy bus journey that would take her to Hachinohe, where she could pick up a bullet train to Tachikawa.

Hiroko came outside to watch her leave – her few possessions barely enough to fill a shoulder bag. They hugged briefly and wordlessly, and Sachiko felt hot tears filling her eyes. She turned her back, and started to walk away. At the end of the street she looked back, and saw Hiroko – a now-distant figure with her hand raised, waving farewell, with the small figure of her son beside her.

Sachiko was full of mixed emotions – she was almost certainly leaving this place forever unless any more bodies were recovered. She resolved to come back for the anniversary of the quake, and join the memorial service for those lost. It was a comforting thought, and made the future seem less terrifyingly open-ended.

Right on time the bus arrived and Sachiko found a seat. She put her small bag between her feet. The doors closed and the bus driver pulled away from the bay. Sachiko watched as Kuji slipped away.

It was a long journey to Tokyo – nearly 400 miles south. Tons of wreckage remained to be cleared from the train tracks, and many lines were still out of service. The roads were surprisingly clear, although the verges were piled high with debris. Scraps of fabric waved forlornly where they had been snagged and reminded her of paper fortunes, bad o-mikuji that had been abandoned. The sky was gunmetal grey, and dirty snow was melting in pockets back from the roadside.

Above the road the land rose: green and impenetrable, and seemingly untouched by the disaster.

The bus was half-empty and Sachiko had an entire row of seats to herself. She passed the journey drifting in and out of sleep, with the daze broken by the occasional jolting of the bus when it hit a crack in the road surface. Once they stopped for 20 minutes, to allow a work team to clear rubble from their path. Sachiko got off the bus and shivered in the dawn chill. Her breath misted the air in front of her. Around her the countryside was quiet – there was barely the call of a bird to break the silence. Along the roadside small trees and bushes were growing, with hardly the promise of leaves in the hard green buds along their branches. It was already April. In happier times she and Harry might have gone to see the cherry blossoms, drinking and carousing with the hundreds that celebrated the cherry blossom fes- tival, *ohanami,* in Sumida Park and laughing at bad jokes and licking *sake* from each other's lips. But nothing had been normal since Tashi. And now – now it seemed as though she would never have the oppor- tunity to fix what had gone wrong between them. She had not cried for them. Now, looking at the hints of spring, latent in the life around her, she felt the grief well and strain against the internal barriers she had so painstakingly created over the days before. And would it be so wrong to give in?

She heard the bus driver calling and, through the haze of tears that blinded her, stumbled back to her seat. It would not be right to wail and scream and rend her hair. All around her was loss – none untouched it seemed. She could feel the strength in their quietness; a steely resolve that was subtle, but unmistakable. Thinking about her life she realised it was something she had grown up with. Her parents had the same quality. Sachiko had forgotten how to find that strength during her time with Harry. She would need it now.

There seemed little point in looking back, in dwelling on what had been. She must look forward and start to plan what would happen next. It was hard to think of the future though. She felt numb, reac- tive, like stone. She looked at the other passengers. There must be others like her: other survivors. It seemed that there should be some way to distinguish them from those whose lives had been but lightly touched by the tsunami. Did she imagine it – was that man there, four seats along, gritting his teeth, his eyes empty, hiding from the knowledge of everything that had been lost? Were those the signs? She started to see them in other faces – there an older woman, closed in on herself, her face haunted.

It was a three-hour onward train journey to Tokyo, through country apparently untouched by any disaster, but gradually filling with factories and industrial complexes. Tokyo, a true conurbation, would swallow them all in its vastness – would swallow her!

What kind of life could she make for herself there?

Part 2

'Japan – the world's only post-atomic society... something that's solidly and uniquely Japanese. When you try to pin that something down though, you realise there's nothing there.'

Ryu Murakami in conversation with Ryuichi Sakamoto, 1985

十五

North-eastern Japan is like another country to a resident of Tokyo – the language is not so different as to be incomprehensible, but it's easy to miss regional subtleties with the strong native accent. When Sachiko had first moved up north, to the village of Taro, she had trouble understanding the local people, with their thick impenetrable consonants, even though they spoke slowly compared to Tokyoites who seemed to rattle through their sentences at top speed. Now that she was back in Tokyo her ears were slowly readjusting to the accent of the city, the cauldron of industry. The first thing she noticed was how fast everyone talked. She should have remembered from her years in Omotesando. She too had been a worker there: commuted daily, put in long hours, had colleagues, friends. That life felt entirely foreign to her now. She had no desire to look up any of the people she had known in those days. After all what would they speak about? Her missing family? She had lost two families now: the one she was born to and the one she had made for herself. It felt like a long way back to the rest of humanity.

Tokyo in April had already shrugged off any signs of winter. The sprawling suburbs shimmered in the noon sun as the train passed through the stations. At first the tracks had seemed to be winding through an endless canyon of steel and concrete, but now the buildings had thinned out and were much lower. Level crossings appeared, with gaggles of uniformed school children, waiting patiently to cross, and the odd rural vehicle. There was an indefinable difference now from the old days, but Sachiko struggled to put her finger on it. Here there was no detritus on the tracks and the low streets looked normal, but all the same it felt almost like something was wrong. She saw many more people than usual with facemasks, even scarves wrapped around their faces, their hands gloved, despite the warmth of the day.

The agency had given her a list of flats to look at near Tachikawa, and she had arranged an appointment at the first address. It was just one more stop. Small fields began to appear between industrial zones and all of a sudden they were at Tachikawa. Sachiko quickly gathered her things and got off. She stood on the platform as the train rushed away and listened to the silence that followed it. She had been the only person to alight at that stop and the station was almost deserted. She was tired and somewhat dazed after the long journey, with that feeling of displacement that travelling by bullet train always gave her. The relatively short journey to Tachikawa had barely provided a buffer between here and the broken towns and villages of the coast. She walked over to the exit, where there was a local map, and compared it to the first of the addresses on the list the agent had sent her. She was looking for an unremarkable apartment block – three floors, twenty or so apartments. She had come to look at a single occupant mansion flat on the second storey. Anonymous enough, she hoped, to be able to start a new life, without being too faceless. She needed to learn to start making connections again. Well – she would see.

Having oriented herself she covered the few streets quickly and was soon at the apartment block. The bottom bell was inscribed with careful characters: 'S & N Takamoto, Caretakers', and she gave it a tentative press. Almost immediately she heard the sound of someone approaching, and the door opened to reveal a well-preserved woman in her seventies wearing a housedress, and smiling.

'You must be Mrs Turnbull? Mr Okagawa said to expect you about now. Come in!'

'Hello! Yes I am, but please call me Sachiko – and you must be Mrs Takamoto? I'm very pleased to meet you.'

Sachiko was a little taken aback at being invited into Mrs Takamoto's home. She had expected to be taken straight to view the apartment. She followed Mrs Takamoto into the building and found herself in a slightly fussy and worn, but perfectly clean, home. Mrs Takamoto pointed her towards a chair, continuing, 'Sit down a moment, dear. I'll just get the book and the keys.'

She vanished into another room whilst Sachiko sat on the very edge of her seat, knees pressed together and back straight, and concentrated on looking respectable. The rent here was very cheap.

Mrs Takamoto bustled back into the room, followed by a man

Sachiko assumed must be her husband. He looked as grumpy as his wife was kind. Sachiko stood up to follow them upstairs to see the apartment, but Mrs Takamoto placed a gentle hand on her shoulder and pressed her back down.

'Wouldn't you like a cup of tea first, dear?'

Her husband burst out, 'You're so bossy. She doesn't want tea – she wants to see the flat. You'll talk her ear off given half a chance. She will you know!'

'Shush you! You don't know what she wants. Don't mind him – he's just a grumpy old man! Off with you now – I'd like a little chat with Sachiko first. Tea, Sachiko?'

Within the gentleness Sachiko sensed a steely resolve, and in Mrs Takamoto's dark eyes she saw a sharp light that knew human beings for what they were. Sachiko had a feeling that Mrs Takamoto had survived more than even she had; old wounds long-healed, but they had made her stronger.

'I couldn't trouble you.'

'No trouble at all, dear. After all, we really should get acquainted if we're going to be neighbours. Are you in a hurry? Young people nowadays are always in a hurry. Life is such a rush. You can hardly catch them from one month to the next! Sit awhile, my dear, tell me about yourself.'

Conscious of making a good impression, Sachiko did. Little by little Mrs Takamoto teased out the whole story, and, as Sachiko told it, she could feel herself lightening, as though she'd cast off some heavy burden from her shoulders.

'And that's when I decided to come back to Tokyo,' she concluded.

Throughout the whole story, Mrs Takamoto had made sympathetic noises and kept Sachiko's teacup refilled. Sachiko had tried not to cry, but couldn't help herself as she told of the days spent searching for any mention of her family, and the bodies she had examined for any likeness to Harry or Tashi. Mrs Takamoto had kept a box of tissues to hand, and supplied them inconspicuously.

'Well, dear, it sounds like you're in search of a refuge. You're not the first woman to need a safe place. Shall I show you the flat now?'

They took the stairs up to the first floor, and Sachiko was presented with a row of identical doors, with potted plants dotted around the corridor between them. Mrs Takamoto stopped outside number nine and fitted a key in the lock, opening the door. She stepped back so that Sachiko could see into the small space.

'It's been empty for a little while. A young man lived here for several years, but he went back to help his family resettle after the tsunami. I've aired it all so it should be nice and fresh. What do you think? Go on in, have a look around.'

As Mrs Takamoto rattled on, Sachiko stepped over the threshold. She noticed that the niche for the household gods was empty, and thought absentmindedly that she should remedy that. She found herself in a small room, with a tiny kitchenette in an alcove off to the side. Even unfurnished the room looked minute; she would have to pick up a chair and a futon. The window was covered by a slatted blind, through which the morning sunlight poured in, and Sachiko walked over to look at the view.

As she gazed down into the unassuming street that reminded her, blessedly, of nothing, she made up her mind.

'I'll take it. It will be perfect.'

'Oh I'm so glad,' enthused Mrs Takamoto, 'I don't like it when parts of the building are empty. It interferes with the balance of things. Wait till I tell Father – he'll be very pleased, although of course he won't show it. Let's pop back downstairs and we can do the paperwork.'

Sachiko had only recently managed to replace the papers that showed where her primary residence was registered. They listed all the places she had lived – with her parents, as a student in halls, as a working woman, as a young bride. And, finally, Taro. Sachiko resolutely stifled the quick pang of pain – those last couple of addresses listed Harry as well.

They went back downstairs to the busy living room, and soon completed the necessary forms. She handed over the key money, the deposit and the first month's rent, and Mrs Takamoto gave her the keys, just as her husband appeared with yet more tea. At being told the news his dour exterior was transformed with a beaming smile.

'Welcome to the neighbourhood! Want me to help you carry your things upstairs?'

'I don't have any more things,' Sachiko admitted, a little shame-facedly, 'just this bag.'

'Now, Father – don't embarrass her, you old fool.' Although her words were harsh, Sachiko could feel the love shared between them. Turning back to Sachiko, Mrs Takamoto continued, 'I'm sure we'll soon have you sorted out with the necessities of life. There's a good yen shop not far from here, and we can lend you some bedding until you get sorted. Is there anything else you need?'

'You've already been too kind,' protested Sachiko, 'I couldn't possibly trouble you more!'

'No trouble at all,' Mrs Takamoto replied, firmly. 'After what you've been through it's the least we can do. Why don't you go and relax for a little while, and I'll send Father up with the bedding shortly. And you must eat with us this evening. I insist!'

Realising that she wouldn't take no for an answer, Sachiko obeyed her instructions, and climbed the stairs to her new apartment. It felt wonderful to be able to close the door behind her, and not to hear the sounds of others through thin walls. To have a window, and a blind, that looked out onto a quiet street, rather than being crowded into temporary accommodation. As she looked out of the window, onto her new neighbourhood, Sachiko felt more content than she had for a long time. Since long before the tsunami – in fact, since long before she and Harry had left Tokyo to move up north, if she was honest with herself. She had a feeling that maybe she could be happy here.

十六

The bell rang, and from the back room Hiromichi heard the shuffle of feet being wiped on his doormat. He dried his hands and walked through – a smile on his face for the customer he hoped would come in and spend some money. These days, all around, there was an air of austerity. Profit warnings, belt-tightening. Doom and gloom. The mood was catching – and if people came into his shop for a little escapism from the present day darkness, who was he to blame them? He was selling a lot more manga. And coffee. Unemployment was up, and sometimes people came to the bookshop just to while away the hours and scour the newspaper over a pot of tea. The classics were suffering.

He stood behind the cash desk, with his hands upon it like a lectern, and beamed at the slight girl who had come in. Outside, it was a blustery and rainy day, and she was windswept and not a little damp and dishevelled.

Sachiko saw a man of perhaps 45 – a man who kept himself trim but was past the first flush of youth. He was smiling at her – a smile that said, 'I want to help you'. She found herself beaming back. It had been a while.

'Hello, can I help you?'

'I'm new around here – I just moved in around the corner yesterday. I'd like to use your web terminal if that's ok?'

'Sure – it's free to customers. Would you like something to eat or drink?'

Sachiko was flustered for a minute – she'd expected it to be a cost per hour. Snacking was the last thing on her mind. She frequently forgot to eat for hours and days at a time. She scanned the menu on the wall behind him, distracted. 'Can I have a hot chocolate please.'

'Coming right up. Take a seat over by the computer table, and I'll bring it over to you when it's ready. You don't need a password to log on, but I will need to see some identification for the log.'

Most people these days came in to use the Wi-Fi – they didn't bother with the old PC. It had the usual browser software on it, but everything slightly out of date. It was creakingly slow. Thus, by the time he had made her drink, and assembled it on the tray with a plate of biscuits, it was just loading the search engine that had been set as the home page.

Hiromichi brought the tray to Sachiko, and set it down near her.

'Thank you! That looks delicious.'

Her voice was soft. Her eyes looked a little haunted; there were dark shadows beneath them that spoke of sleepless nights.

'Do you need any help with the computer? Sorry it's not the fastest. Most people come in here with laptops or use their phone.'

'I'll be fine thanks.'

'Ok well shout if you need anything. I'll be just over here.'

Sachiko nodded, her fingers already calling up her webmail. She fired off a quick message to Hiroko, with her new address, and deleted the junk mails that filled her inbox. No news from the Taro relief organisation. Reconstruction was continuing. No bodies had been recovered that week. Automatically she flipped to a news site. As the pages slowly loaded on the ancient computer her mind went over the same ground again and again. She'd been here before. There was never any news. She needed something to take her mind off all of this. Something to fill her days. And she would need work, but she wasn't quite ready to think about that yet.

Sachiko shut down the browser and sat, sipping her hot chocolate and nibbling the biscuits. Her eyes scanned the shelves around her. The space was set up as a bookshop and café, and felt like a cosy and pleasant place to be. Bookcases lined the walls, with handwritten notes below featured editions adding a personal touch to the selection. It had been a long time since Sachiko had read any books – although she had once loved reading. She had lost the ability to concentrate on a book when she was pregnant, and even before that she had avoided reading books in Japanese. Harry didn't like her disappearing into a world he couldn't enter. She stood and wandered over to the fiction section. There were the classics, European works in translation and books by Japanese authors, young and old.

A thick volume caught her eye and she slid it from the shelf. *Col-*

lected Modern Stories. Opening it she scanned the contents and saw stories by writers she remembered and others new to her. She closed the book and checked the price on the back cover. She had that much on her, just about. Maybe a good book was what she needed to take her out of herself for a while.

Hiromichi watched her, subtly, from where he was stocktaking by the till, as she stood absorbed in a book she had found in the fiction section. There was something in the sloppy-vintage style of her dress, the way that she held herself, that made her seem impossibly fragile and strong at the same time – like a delicate vase wrought from steel. Although obviously Japanese, she had a foreign air about her. It was as if she was dancing in a bubble, untouchable.

Sachiko went back to the table where she'd left her bag. The hot chocolate had gone cold; only a few crumbs remained of the biscuits. She picked up the bag and went over to the counter to pay.

'That was delicious – thanks. Can I have this too please?'

She held out the book and he put a hand out to take it, checked the price, rang it up.

'A great choice – this collection's just come out. Is it for you, or a friend?'

'It's for me – no need to gift-wrap it. The news is so bad these days I'd rather lose myself in fiction for a while.'

'I don't blame you!' Hiromichi replied, with feeling. 'That'll be nine hundred yen. Thanks so much!'

'Bye! See you soon!'

And just like that she was gone.

I am in the present. I watch the walls around, garish with video feeds. Again and again, waves crash over insufficient defences: sweeping away cars and buildings; crushing boats like matchstick models; shattering concrete. People run, their mouths form tiny 'O's, silent screams. The images are grainy, pixelated. They repeat and overlap each other, so that there is barely a square centimetre of wall that isn't covered, and everywhere the same stories are repeated. Rows of bodies await collection. The debris of lives litters city streets. All these images are burned on my frozen retinas until I can take no more; my ears are full of the white noise of destruction.

A whitish-blue and flickering light covers everything in the room. I try not to see the images, but it's as if my eyelids have been surgically excised; I can't shut them out. I concentrate on trying to reconstruct the narrative that brought me here. The strands have unwoven in my mind and I can't seem to remember what led to this moment. What am I doing here? Where am I?

I concentrate on touch. My fingers are clenched, elbows tucked between my knees; my head turned at an uncomfortable angle. Now I concentrate on unclenching a finger. Then another. I make my hand flat, force it to stroke the rough surface of the old blanket upon which I lie. The blanket is made of wool – maybe that of a goat, or a sheep. I focus all my attention on those fingers, to close out the images all around me.

I had fled from the tsunami. But there was something before that. A family. A child. All around me the endless diorama continues, fragmenting everything. What happened? How did I end up here? I remember flight. I feel relief that I survived. I am alive. The flickering continues. I will the disaster to be over. Enough already. They are gone. I can't help them now.

'Now, now, Papa – what a terrible thing to think. Don't you feel sorry for all these poor people? Look how they suffer – and what's your reaction? You try to shut it out, to pretend that they never existed. And, after all, what's the fate of a few thousand Japanese people to you? You've always considered yourself superior – ever since you started reading a few books in translation and decided you were some kind of expert on Japanese culture. Just another weeaboo kid who thinks Japan is so great.'

It's him. The child – but I thought he was gone and how can he be back?

'Don't try to pretend you can't see me. Someone is going to pay for what happened to me. And it's not going to be her, is it? The insanity defence? Please, I mean really! What court in the land is going to buy that? Eventually they're going to work out how I died, and you've made yourself look so very guilty by running away. The penalty for murder is death in Japan. And I was only a child. That will increase the gravity of the crime.'

I lie there listening to the words that roll on inexorably, providing a background to the silent cinema. I should know what the voice is talking about; it's part of the fractured narrative. Maybe if I watch the walls it will all make sense; somewhere amongst the images will be the story I left behind. But I can hardly bring myself to look.

I press an exploring hand to the bed, and bring the other hand around to meet it. I could bring my knees in, and swing my body around just so, and sit up. I think it, but it is as if thought and action are on parallel courses, destined never to meet; the link between intention and movement severed. My body will not obey.

'Look at you – *kuzu*! It's bad enough running away from your responsibilities, but now you're going to lie there wallowing in your own self-pity. You make me sick.'

I rest my head back on the blanket and stare at the beams above me. Blue light flickers over their edges and occasionally lights up dark corners. Faces flash up, distorted by the uneven surfaces, so I am aware of little more than random features; hands reaching; eyes dark with loss. Children peep fearfully from behind the knees of their carers. Small groups of people wait on their rooftops for rescue. Waves destroy bridges, roads, houses, villages. Tiny matchbox cars race against the oncoming waves, only to be caught and tossed like toys in a bathtub. Tugs and fishing boats slam into the shore, crushing everything in their path. Sea walls crumble. Tilt shift; the tiny figures grow and swell about me as if I'm diving into close focus. I can't take it any more. I force my eyes shut.

'Harry?'

'Yes, darling?'

'I've found us a lovely place in Taro. Let's go and see it tomorrow.'

'I can't do tomorrow, Sachiko – I'll be teaching. Can't we go on Saturday?'

'I suppose so. I just want to get it settled. Are you sure you still want to move up north?'

'Of course I'm sure. But I can't afford to lose this job now, or risk a bad reference – not if you want to move before the baby comes.'

We were both silent and I noticed Sachiko stroking her belly. At 16 weeks she was starting to get a noticeable bump, and I wasn't yet used to the changes in her – the thickening of her body that was starting to make bending difficult. She who had always been so graceful was becoming unwieldy. There hadn't been any movement yet.

Baby. Person. New being in our life; it was an odd concept, even though we had talked about it – and decided to embark on parenthood together.

'I guess Saturday would be fine. I'll call Ichimura-san and ask him if that will be ok for him.'

'Well, I hope so. I don't think I'll be able to get the time off work before then. Now if you don't mind I'd like to try to get a little writing done before I'm too tired to think straight. If I can concentrate after teaching all day long. Have you been out at all today?'

'Yes of course I have. I went out to get the greens for dinner.'

'So you did. Well, it looks like it's a lovely evening. Why don't you pop out and get some fresh air? Fresh air is supposed to be good for people in your condition isn't it? Only I'd love a bit of peace and quiet. Why don't you give Michiko a call and ask if she wants to meet up?'

'I haven't seen Michiko for months. We've got nothing in common any more. And anyway I don't want to go out now. There's nothing I need to do; no one I need to see. And I need to finish putting these dishes away.'

'I suppose they weren't the right type of friends for you. Anyway we'll have our own family soon. You won't miss them.

'I got a letter back from the high school in Taro today – they made me a formal offer of the teaching role. Are you sure you still want to do this?'

She continued drying the dishes slowly and carefully.

'Harry, you're not happy here and you want to write. Why would I stand in your way? Taro seems like a lovely place. I'm sure we'll soon get to know people there. And babies are great for breaking the ice with new people. It will be fine.'

'Well, I'm glad to hear you sounding so optimistic. It's exactly what I need – to get out of this rat race and into the real Japan. I can't wait to get writing there!'

'Yes. I'm sure you'll produce some of your best work.'

Although her words were encouraging, there was a surprising bitterness in her tone. I'd never expected marriage to be an easy ride, but somehow recently it seemed we were often on the brink of a silent war. Sachiko had always been reserved, but it had felt like there was an innocence and sweetness in her when we first met that I rarely saw now, even though she was outwardly thoughtful and kind. We were both quiet for a little while.

'Harry, it moved! I felt something!'

'Really? Where? You're sure it wasn't wind?'

'I'm sure. It didn't feel anything like that. It was definitely a wiggle!'

In a moment I was behind her, with my two hands cupping her stomach. Minutes passed, but I couldn't feel any movement from the baby.

'Teasing little bugger isn't he?'

'What a charming little scene, Papa. So kind of you to invite me. It's not every day you get to see what your parents were like before you were born. So, did you ever like each other? Quite the little cold war you two had going on there.'

'It wasn't always like that!' I found myself shouting. 'You're twisting the past! You don't know anything about how it was between us.'

'You didn't know, more like. You'll never be a writer until you learn to read people a bit better. You were never able to read her! Even before she hid away from you, she was already far gone. Do you know why? Do you know what you did to her with your constant assumption of superiority? You were just acting out the old story;

the one that never changes. She gave up talking to you because you scorned everything she tried to share with you.'

Relentless. He is there, always there, gloating at me, and, behind him, the show goes on, the carnival of horrors. A 24-hour news channel on repeat; all the news channels layered over each other until nothing else is visible, projected somehow on every surface, like wraparound television screens on the walls, the ceiling, the floor. Everywhere I look, destruction. Could there have been that much destruction? How much of the coast was obliterated? The clips are changing. Mixed in with the crushing waves I see giant helicopters, airlifting water. Concrete bunkers, swarming with emergency vehicles and white-suited figures. Are those radiation suits? I remember Tashi mentioning Fukushima – those early updates.

Over all this, live feeds hug the rafters – a scrolling stream of text updating with the numbers of the lost, the latest disasters. I close my eyes and try to take refuge in my memories again. But the distance won't come; the present intrudes in the form of Tashi. I put my fingers in my ears, like a child, but I can still hear him.

'*Papa*, it's so boring when you ignore me. Can't you just give me that? All my short life I've been ignored.'

It's no good. I have to answer him.

'Ignored? How could we ignore you when you never stopped crying? You weren't ignored – you became the centre of our life. We couldn't avoid you.'

'That's my whole point. You endured me, but you never loved me. She didn't either. When I needed her to be there she was absent, and then worse than absent. You failed to protect me. How could you do that to me?'

'Leave me alone. You're not even real. Ghosts don't exist. It's just my mind.'

'If that's the case how can I leave you alone? Surely that's your choice? Maybe you really want me to stick around?'

I don't answer. I don't know. I don't know anything any more.

十八

The next time she came into the shop it was raining again. Hiromichi heard the doorbell tinkling and looked up from where he was arranging some new arrivals on a low side table. She had no umbrella, and her hair was loosely twisted in a western-style bun. In fact there was the same careless grace about her that had so struck him on her first visit. Drops of rainwater sparkled on her soft skin and he could tell she wore no make-up. This time it was she that spoke first.

'Hi! Good to see you again. I've come back to use your Internet connection again, and was wondering if you could recommend me a good book to read?'

'Certainly – I'd be more than happy to! I'll see what I can come up with whilst you're on the computer.'

Sachiko quickly filled out the Internet access register and took the same seat as last time in front of the ancient monitor. Of course she could have bought a cheap netbook from some electronics store in Akihabara, but she didn't know much about computers and was still far too short of money for any major purchases. Then, too, she liked this bookshop and had a good feeling about the owner.

She had enjoyed the collection she had bought last time. At first she had devoured it, jumping straight from one story to the next without pause for thought, but towards the end she had forced herself to slow down, to pause between stories and think about them. They had allowed her to reconnect with Japanese writing. All of Harry's books had been Western classics, and in her attempts to get more fluent at English she hadn't bothered to keep up with Japanese fiction. There was a kind of honesty and directness to the new fiction that she found compelling. She liked that hint of the surreal; of subversion – whether it was in ordinary things becoming strange, or characters creating their own fantastic universes, religions and histories. The only constant was the unexpected, keeping things off balance. This was in some ways the most seditious aspect of the more modern stories. Most importantly, she had been able to forget the present whilst reading them. She craved any kind of escape from the now, and from her memories.

With a whirring and a clicking that sounded slightly ominous, the monitor lit up, and the search page flickered onto the screen.

Sachiko wrote a quick email to Hiroko to ask if she was still waiting to be rehoused and fill her in on what she'd been up to. The second was a short message to the rescue centre, requesting that they send any news about Harry and Tashi to her new address. By now she felt this was going through the motions. She didn't believe that they would ever be found alive. But there was still a slim chance that their bodies might be recovered and she could finally lay them to rest. The hardest part had been not being able to make the proper ceremonies as each seven days had passed. The rituals, according to Shinto belief would help their spirits pass out of this realm and be reborn. She wondered if that also applied to Harry, who had been born a Christian, but had embraced atheism with the dogmatism of one who needed some kind of faith, but couldn't bring himself to believe that others had found it. Were they even now wandering as ghosts?

With all her correspondence complete, she logged off the computer. The shopkeeper was nowhere to be seen, so she walked over to the low table he had been arranging when she came in. On it he had placed a selection of books of short stories from writers throughout the previous century, each with a short introductory card hand-labelled in a clear and neat script. Akutagawa, Shusako Endo, Ango Sakaguchi. Some of those names were familiar, and she had read a little of their work, but others were strange to her. She reached for a book of tales by Sakaguchi and opened it at random. She was immediately absorbed – transported back through the decades, to the mountains and a time when ghosts were a common feature of Japanese life.

One line particularly struck her, and seemed to draw a parallel with her own life, with the way she had been before the tsunami: 'Wrapped in a cold silent wind that never moved… he'd feel the life inside him scattering like so many soft silent cherry blossoms.' It seemed to capture that exact feeling of being suspended outside time; the emptiness that started as a haven and became a prison. The story was called 'In the Forest, Under Cherries in Full Bloom' and as she read she was

struck by how subtle the writing was – so different from the literature that Harry had introduced her to. As she was reading, Hiromichi
came back into the shop from the back room.

'Ah – I see you've discovered Ango Sakaguchi. I was going to ask
which writers you were interested in. Do you know much about his
work?'

'No, nothing,' Sachiko replied truthfully. 'We read some of the
classics at school, but that was a long time ago.'

'Well, Sakaguchi's not a bad place to start. He had a unique vision.'

Sachiko paid for the book, whilst Hiromichi wrapped it up.

'Will there be anything else?'

'Not today,' Sachiko replied, 'but I'm sure I'll be back soon.'

'Do let me know what you think. It's not so many people that are
interested in the classics nowadays – so it always makes me happy
when someone comes in and gives a book like this one a good home.'

'Thank you – I surely will. Maybe I'll even write you a little book
report. I've got plenty of spare time at the moment.'

Hiromichi chuckled at her joke.

'Thanks – I'll look forward to receiving it. See you soon I hope.
Arigato gozaimashita.'

Taking the neatly wrapped parcel, Sachiko turned to leave the shop.
At the door she paused as if to ask something, and then changed her
mind and left with a wave. Hiromichi watched her go and thought
once again there was something indefinably attractive about her. It
was a feeling he had not experienced for a long time, and he hoped
that she would be back again soon; it was too long since he had someone to talk to.

十九

Sachiko could feel herself slowly recovering. Her days had fallen into a predictable pattern, and she began to feel that her wounds were healing. She spent most of her mornings in the bookshop chatting to Hiromichi about literature, and her afternoons with Mrs Takamoto at the apartment block. Sadly she knew that this state of affairs could not continue indefinitely; living on her own was expensive, and the emergency compensation money would be stopping soon. She would have to get a job.

She reviewed all the options open to her. Clerical work; going back to publishing – but she wanted her days free to build on the fragile relationships that were helping her to remain human. That left night work; and, unless she wanted to become a factory worker, that meant waitressing in the centre – either Ginza or Roppongi. She tried to imagine how that would make her feel. Serving drinks to businessmen. Their inevitable suggestions. What if they wanted a little more? Well, she was probably too old anyway, at 32, to work in a place like that.

That afternoon Sachiko took the train into the centre of Tokyo for the first time in several weeks. Living in Tachikawa, with nothing to fill her days but wandering the quiet residential streets, she had adapted to a slower pace of life. Tokyo station felt fast, hectic and incredibly crowded to her. She transferred to the metro and got off at Ginza, then started to scope out the shops and bars. Which to choose? But it was no good. There was no way she'd get a job in any of these places. For a start she'd need a new wardrobe. Impossible, when she could barely afford to feed herself and pay her rent.

Wandering the gridded streets, with their smart shops and immaculate window displays, she felt dowdy and underdressed. The months up north, followed by weeks in the outskirts of Tokyo, had caused her to forget how sculpted and perfect the women of Tokyo were. Sachiko was always clean and neat, but rarely wore makeup and didn't follow fashion. Here she saw women tottering on unfeasibly high heels, shopping bags hooked over their elbows, manicured nails gleaming, meeting for coffee in chic cafés. Uniformed staff bowed low as they passed and offered their wares in sing-song voices, and Sachiko felt even more invisible when they failed to bow to her. Windows were conspicuously void of 'staff wanted' signs. And anyway, could she do that kind of work? Maybe she'd be better off getting a job as a cleaner or a carer for now. It had been naïve of her to think she could slot straight back into city life. There seemed little prospect of work here.

Sachiko kept walking. Soon she found herself heading towards Shinjuku. Here were Westerners, gawping at the neon logos, faint in the daylight; garish signs fighting for attention and advertising Girls! Irish bar! Bustling arcades packed with titty bars, phone shops and love hotels jostling cheek by jowl with shrines and office blocks. An endless stream of people walked past and Sachiko knew that there was little for her here. The press of people only made her feel lonelier. It started to rain, and she had not thought to bring an umbrella out with her.

She quickened her step, heading for Koenji – there at least she would be able to find a cheap and filling supper at one of the fast food places near the station, and it wasn't too far. She could take the train back to the suburbs from there – the afternoon spent in the city had tired her out; the miles covered creating an empty and hollow feeling in her belly. Despite her sensible shoes, her feet were weary.

She followed the JR train line between Shinjuku and Koenji, relishing the quiet beneath the massive concrete pilings of the railway above. Here was a whole ecosystem flourishing in the eternal shade cast by the suspended tracks. Hundreds of bikes were parked in the pockets created there, and warehouses and small factories made use of the blocks between them. Soon enough she came to Okubo, and not long after heard the melodious tones that meant Nakano station was overhead. It was something that she had always taken for granted, but Harry had been charmed that each station on the subway system had its own tune. It had started as an aid for blind people, but had attained cult status, and you could even buy souvenir trains at each station that played the station jingle. Harry had owned several, before. She had forgotten about them until now.

The rain continued, but Sachiko was protected from the drops as she strolled along. After the haughtiness of Ginza and the madness of Shinjuku she felt a sense of peace begin to descend on her. Quiet and low-rise residential streets stretched and wound to the right and left of her, their inhabitants at work or school. Occasionally she passed an elderly person sweeping and washing their front steps. People inclined their heads in greeting, but otherwise ignored her as she passed, their hands busy with brushes and mops. The rain was easing and the streets looked new-washed, glinting in the sudden sunlight that broke from between the clouds. Oil glinted in unexpected rainbows from the gutters and she heard the plaintive tones of a cat in heat.

As she neared Koenji the undercroft was replaced by a quiet arcade lined with tiny *izakaya*, standing bars advertising dinner and snacks for a few hundred yen. Sachiko was reminded of her empty belly and stopped at the third place she passed – a narrow little bar with room for maybe six customers. She had been here with Harry when they first met. She sat at the high counter and ordered *udon*, and within moments a bowl of steaming noodles was before her. She remembered with a pang how Harry had always been surprised at the speed with which food was served in Japan. He said it was far superior to those surly English cafés where a 'quick' meal could take 20 minutes or more to arrive.

As she worked her way through the *udon*, Sachiko reviewed her options. The trip into Tokyo had reminded her why she had been keen to leave – it was as though she saw it with new eyes. There was little for her here she sensed – but then, without Harry and Tashi, what was there for her anywhere? Maybe she should have stayed up north and helped with the clean-up effort. There was still a lot to be done, she knew, to remove the clinging mud and wreckage, and rebuild lives shattered by the tsunami that had swept away so many communities along the coast.

On the wall a flat screen television was playing the news, with the volume on low. Two announcers were talking about the crisis in

Fukushima – set to be the worst nuclear power disaster the world had ever seen, even exceeding Chernobyl. The authorities were still battling to control the core, which was pumping out radioactive water into the sea, and the outlook looked grim both for the power station, and for the thousands of people who had had to evacuate their homes. Sachiko wondered if they'd ever be able to return – and what the impact of seawater thousands of times above safe radiation levels would have on the local wildlife. Fukushima had always been one of her favourite provinces – with beautiful national parks and a thriving city at its heart. It saddened her to think how much of the area was now uninhabitable. And was it true, what people were saying, that the situation was actually much worse than the government was willing to let on?

Oh, the present was just unbearable! Her mind drifted back to the times she had come here with Harry in the old days.

They had come to eat udon *beneath the underpass, where you could get great steaming bowls of noodles served in broth for five hundred yen. She often ate in places like this. They weren't fancy and you knew exactly what you were getting. Wax models, their shine dulled by a thin patina of dust, advertised the dishes on their menu. The best places only had three or four, and the food, when it came, was exactly like the model. She had ordered for both of them, and within moments they were presented with bowls of noodles and broth, garnished with prawn tempura and greens.*

'Why are you giggling, Sachiko? Have I got something on my face?'

'No – nothing – but you can't eat them like that!'

'Eat what like what?'

'Your noodles. You're not supposed to pick them up with your chopsticks and blow on them – here's how you do it.'

Sachiko demonstrated, slurping them up noisily straight from the bowl. Harry was a bit shocked. Sachiko usually seemed so demure and polite.

'You'd never get away with eating like that in a restaurant in England.'

'Well, that's how we do it here. It shows you're enjoying them and it cools them down too. Try it!'

Harry tried to copy Sachiko – using both chopsticks and soup spoon to slurp the noodles up.

'Actually you're right – it does make more sense this way. And also explains why I always end up with a bowl of half-cold broth at the end.'

'See – I told you so.'

They continued eating, Sachiko sneaking glances at Harry in between mouthfuls. He looked so earnest. She couldn't tell if he was genuinely enjoying the udon, or if he just wanted to please her.

'Do you like them then?'

'Yes – I really do – they're much nicer this way. But I think that's probably the company too. It's great being with you. I'm really starting to feel like I'm seeing Japan from the inside. You're a great guide, Sachiko.'

Sachiko blushed. It didn't seem so much, and it was fun experiencing the world through Harry's eyes. She could never tell what would strike him as strange.

'I'm enjoying being with you too. I can't believe this is only the third time we've met. It feels like we've known each other for much longer.'

It was true. Once she'd got over the strangeness of him not being Japanese, she felt very comfortable with Harry.

Now he was exaggerating the slurping, sucking up great mouthfuls of udon and smacking his lips. She laughed.

'The chef will be very pleased you like his food so much.'

'Good. I do like it. I like everything you're showing me, Sachiko. I want to see, and taste, and feel a lot more.'

As he looked at her, his blue eyes earnest over his noodle bowl, Sachiko realised he was telling her he was ready for their relationship to move on. And she was ready too. She smiled back.

'And I can't wait to show you some more. Come on – let's get going. There's a lot more to see!'

Sachiko shook her head and dragged herself back to now. It had been such a beautiful time. They had been so young. It felt like they could do anything, like the whole world was there for them. And in a different way, that was exactly where she had ended up now. There were no ties; no one expected anything of her. She was poised on the edge of a precipice, and she didn't know what was on the other side. Or indeed if she would even make it across.

Sachiko suddenly had a yen for a cold and frothy glass of beer, but there was no way she could afford to drink out on her budget – not with the prices of beer in Tokyo. Even vending machine beer was almost out of her range – she had to watch every yen now. She really needed a job, but it looked as though the afternoon spent in Tokyo city had been in vain. Maybe she could learn to be a cook?

Paying up, she left the cosy noodle bar to continue her walk. Up ahead she could hear the sound of buskers. The sound both cheered and saddened her; she had come here with Harry in the old days, to poke around the vintage shops and listen to live music at the Mission bar.

Those days seemed very far away now. The Harry that she had lost was a very different person to the one she had fallen in love with – had it really been almost 10 years before? A selfish and insensitive stranger had replaced that carefree and chivalrous Englishman; one who subsumed everything in the service of his own passions. Maybe she had been foolish to throw her lot in with a foreigner, who could never truly understand Japanese ways. Her mind turned involuntarily to Hiromichi. He hadn't said anything, but she got the impression that he liked her. Sachiko knew that he would never broach the subject, but found herself wondering what she would say if he did.

二十

The next morning dawned bright and clear. Sachiko woke early, stretched luxuriously, and contemplated the day that lay ahead. The trip to Tokyo yesterday had been something of a waste of time. She ought to have realised that you couldn't just walk into the nearest bar and get a job. Most of them weren't even advertised – people just asked their friends if they knew someone suitable and would always hire someone they knew over a stranger. Sachiko realised that she'd been rather naïve. But then, sheltered by her education, her family and friends she hadn't really noticed how hard life could be. She'd never really been alone, she realised, in all her 32 years. She'd gone from schoolgirl to university student, and then fallen into a job in publishing without ever really having to think about what would happen next – it had all come to her, with the help of her parents and teachers. Now, for the first time ever, she had to think for herself.

She could always give in and go back to her parents. That's what anyone else would do in her situation. And no one would judge her harshly for it. In fact, in isolating herself this way she was being most un-Japanese. People would say that the *gaijin* had corrupted her, had broken her connection to her *uchi*, her home. Even now she knew her parents assumed that she would grow out of her rebellion. How could she explain that it wasn't a phase? She was just expressing herself for the first time. Meeting Harry had made her realise how passive she had been all her life – had made her want to be strong and independent just like him.

Well, that hadn't worked out so well it seemed. Maybe independent people only appeared so, but in fact were just intrinsically selfish. Maybe it was time she rejoined the human race.

She decided to go and see Hiromichi-san at the bookshop. If nothing else he might be able to give her some advice about what work to do. It couldn't hurt, and, she had to admit to herself, it would make her happy to see his calm and homely face.

She walked the short distance to the shop and hesitated for a moment in front of the door before squaring her shoulders and pushing it open. The bell tinkled and she saw Hiromichi in his usual position behind the counter. He looked up from the column of figures and the calculator that he'd been working with and a smile split his face.

'Ah! Sachiko-san! Come to continue your education in Japanese literature? You can't have finished that latest collection already. You do read fast!'

'Good morning! No, I haven't finished it yet, although I am enjoying it a lot. I came to see you for some advice actually.'

'Really? And what can I do for you today, Sachiko?'

Sachiko liked the way that he said her name, so easy and natural it tripped off his tongue. Harry had never been able to pronounce it quite right – which at first she had found charming and foreign. Latterly it had bothered her though, just as so much about him had started to. Emboldened by Hiromichi's positive response she continued.

'Hiromichi-san, I really need to find a job. I was wondering if you might have any ideas for me, or know anyone that's looking.'

'What kind of a job?'

'Anything, really, I'm not too fussy. Although something in the afternoons and evenings would be good. I'm really enjoying having a bit of time to study, but as you know life in Tokyo isn't cheap.'

'It's not cheap at all! I wish I could afford to hire you here – but people don't buy as many books as they used to. Sometimes I worry that I'll have to shut up shop and get some other work to make ends meet. What work did you do… before?'

Sachiko wasn't sure if he meant before the tsunami, or before her marriage, and if that had been the reason for the slight pause. Politely, she ignored it and answered his question as honestly as she could.

'I worked for a small publishing house – editorial assistant on a business magazine. It was very dull! Still it was a good job, and one my parents were happy with. I can't really go back there though – even if my position were still open, it's not the kind of job that would work for me now. I'm after something a little more casual – you know that culture of late hours, having to be the first one in the office and the last to leave. It's so pressured. I couldn't do that now. And I'm too old to start again at the bottom of the ladder. It's hard to go back into that kind of stuff. You know what I mean?'

'Not personally,' Hiromichi replied with a smile. 'I inherited this bookshop from my father, and it's the only job I've ever had. Luckily it's a job that I love, so I've never resented it.'

'It must feel very secure, continuing the family business. My mother left her job when she had me and I never had any thought of following my father into a company. Of course, he's retired now and living with my mother in Osaka. Or at least they were. I haven't been in touch for a while.'

Sensing that Hiromichi was disconcerted by hearing such personal information, Sachiko quickly backtracked.

'Anyway – listen to me babbling on. I'm sorry – you don't need to know all of this stuff.'

'Don't worry – the more I know about you, the easier it will be to suggest something that might work. Hmm… I wonder… how about doing it this way. What would you *not* like to do?'

'Well, I'm not really strong enough for manual labour. I could be a waitress – or even a cleaner. I could be a companion for someone elderly. Just something to pay the bills. My English is quite good too. Maybe I could put a card up? Advertise for a "position wanted"?'

'Sure – that could work. I could even write you a reference if you like. Obviously we don't know each other that well, but your excellent literary taste suggests you're of good character.'

Again his face was split by a merry grin, and Sachiko couldn't help smiling back. When Hiromichi saw her smile he was reminded of the first time she had come into the bookshop – the careless grace of her. He felt his ears flush, and was glad that his hair was a little long and concealed them. He hoped his feelings didn't show on his face. He wished things were different so that he could invite her out for supper or a movie. That at least was what people did when they went out on a date – but he didn't know if that was the kind of thing that Sachiko liked. He longed to find out more about her – what went on behind her quiet eyes.

Hiromichi wasn't doing quite such a good job of concealing his feelings as he thought. Sachiko saw the telltale flush and abruptly realised that Hiromichi might have feelings for her too. She wondered how shocked he'd be if she asked him out on a date. Maybe they could go out as friends? Sachiko felt confused. Here she was, ostensibly come to ask advice on how to find a job, only to realise that all along she'd had an ulterior motive that even she wasn't aware of.

They looked at each other for a few moments, neither certain what to do next. Sachiko cleared her throat of the lump that had appeared in it, and strove to keep her voice normal.

'That would be very kind. Ok – I'll go home and write an ad right now! Thanks so much for all the advice. You've given me a lot to think about.'

'That's ok – I'm happy to help. *Ganbatte kudasai!*'

As Sachiko left the shop, Hiromichi cursed himself a little for his shyness. However, he'd been there a long time. He realised that for years he had lived a solitary lifestyle. The possibility of a relationship had never even occurred to him. He would need a while to get used to these unfamiliar feelings. It was probably wise to let things take their own time.

二一

Sachiko gazed out of her window at the driving rain. It had been falling solidly for hours now, and showed no signs of abating. The streets were even more deserted than usual – just the occasional person scurrying past with their umbrella held low, so that from above she could hardly tell whether they were male or female.

The rain was disheartening. It made her feel trapped, and deprived her of one of the few distractions she had in Tokyo: wandering the city streets. Although she tried not to dwell on them, she couldn't rid herself of her feelings of guilt about Tashi. Through her neglect she had murdered him just as surely as though she had done it with her own bare hands. She found herself sitting for hours trying to picture his face. Try as she might his features vanished into the haze of those early months of depression. She couldn't bring them to mind.

It still didn't make sense, that day. She wished she could remember more, and that the days before it weren't also a blank. Maybe Harry had taken Tashi for a walk to calm him. He had cried and cried until they were driven to distraction. It seemed as though he were always in pain. The nurses at the hospital said he was just a colicky baby, that it would pass; but those first months had seemed to stretch out forever.

The time passed slowly, but inexorably – and she still didn't have a job. There had been no response yet to the handwritten card that she had put in the window of Hiromichi's shop. She decided to go downstairs and see if Mrs Takamoto was in. She was always willing to lend a sympathetic ear, and might have some advice for Sachiko. The situation was getting somewhat desperate now… she could afford the next month's rent, but after that she would be homeless unless she could find some more funds from somewhere. Soon she would have no choice but to return to her parents' house in Osaka. As she still hadn't contacted them since the tsunami, she wasn't sure what reception she would receive. Of course, had they checked, they could easily track her down to her current address. The fact that she hadn't heard anything from them could mean that either they hadn't thought to do this, or hadn't wanted to. She suspected it was probably the latter; which made going 'home' an unappealing prospect. She wasn't sure if she had the emotional energy to bridge the rift that had opened between them.

Sliding back the door, she slid her feet into her house slippers and descended the single flight of stairs down to the ground floor. Mrs Takamoto's door was slightly ajar, which meant that she was home – unsurprising in the driving rain. It was the kind of weather that would keep anyone except the desperate indoors. Sachiko knocked gently and a moment later was rewarded with the sight of Mrs Takamoto's smiling face.

'Sachiko-san – what a pleasure! Rain keeping you at home today then?'

'Yes – it's horrible! I hope I'm not imposing? I was feeling a little solitary, and wondered if you might have time for a cup of tea?'

'Of course, my dear. It's lovely to see you. In fact, I was just saying to Father that I hadn't seen you for a couple of days. Come in and have a seat.'

Sachiko took a seat on the low sofa, whilst Mrs Takamoto disappeared through into the small kitchen next door. She could hear the sound of the gas being fired up and the kettle filled, as well as the clattering that meant that Mrs Takamoto was assembling an afternoon snack to accompany the tea. Sachiko knew that there was no point protesting against her kindness. Since she had arrived, no one had come to visit the old couple as far as she was aware. There were photos of a young man and a woman at various stages of growing up scattered on the sideboard and hanging on the walls of the living room. She wondered where they were now. Where once children had held filial respect as a virtue, it had now become unfashionable, and often, as soon as they'd been able to escape the family home, they deserted their parents, limiting their visits to major festivals, rather than the once-mandatory weekly visits. Sachiko hadn't been any different. Now, seeing how lonely these old folk were, she felt pangs of guilt at her treatment of her parents. They hadn't been in the best of health last time she had seen them, and she wondered if they were even still alive. Her father would be in his late seventies now, and her mother wasn't much younger.

Mrs Takamoto came back into the room bearing a tray with tea things and plates of snacks, and laid it down on the low table in front of the sofa.

'Now before you protest that you're not hungry and I shouldn't have taken the trouble to make you anything to eat, I was feeling a bit peckish myself – so you're doing me a favour giving me the chance to have an afternoon snack.'

'I wouldn't dream of protesting.'

Mrs Takamoto settled herself, arranged the tea things, and ceremoniously poured them each a cup. She waited until Sachiko had picked up her tea and then fixed her with a sharp eye.

'So tell me what's wrong today, Sachiko. What's the problem, eh? Are you feeling lonely?'

'Not lonely, no – in fact I love this area. And any time I'm feeling the need for some distraction I can pop down to the bookshop. The problem is that I need to find a job – but I'm not sure where to start, or what kind of job to look for.'

'What did you do... before?'

'I worked in a small publishing house in Omotesando. But that's not really an option now. You could say I burned my bridges when I left.'

That was an understatement. Her resignation letter had been highly critical of the company, and the mindset of the people that worked there, referring to them as 'worker drones'. The letter had perhaps been worded somewhat too strongly – but it was all part of her embracing Harry's culture, at the expense of her own. She realised Mrs Takamoto was looking at her quizzically, a single eyebrow raised.

'Anyway, I don't want to go back to that, not really. I'm after something a little more casual.'

'Well, if it's casual work you're after, I think that shouldn't be too hard. Permanent work is a little harder to come by these days. What are your talents?'

Mrs Takamoto gazed at Sachiko over the rim of her teacup.

Sachiko didn't answer immediately. It felt a little bit like a job interview, and good practice for what she'd surely have to undergo if she actually managed to find a position that sounded like it might suit her. It was a good question and made her realise that she really needed to imagine herself in a job before she'd be able to put herself in that place.

'I thought maybe I could do something like cleaning? Or keeping someone company? My English isn't too bad... but I don't think I'd be very good at teaching.'

'What about nursery work? I read in the paper that there's a big shortage of nursery staff.'

Seeing Sachiko's face fall, Mrs Takamoto was immediately all apologies. 'I'm sorry, that was insensitive of me, with everything that's happened recently. Are you sure you're ready to go back to work?'

'I haven't got a choice. My savings are nearly finished. And I don't want to leave here. It's been such a hard year and I need some stability in my life.'

'I can understand that. I wish I could let you stay here for free, but we don't own the building. We're just caretakers here. Well, there must be something we can do. Let's take a walk to the local shop and have a look in the situations vacant in the newspaper. At least that will give us a place to start.'

'That's too kind of you – and I know you must be busy.'

Mrs Takamoto quieted Sachiko's protests.

'Nonsense. I need a couple of things for dinner, or Shinji will never let me hear the end of it. Let's walk together. The rain seems to have let up a little bit, so it's a good time to go out. Do you need an umbrella?'

'I'll go upstairs and get mine.'

By the time Sachiko came back downstairs Mrs Takamoto had cleared up the tea things, and was standing by the door waiting for her. Outside the rain still came down in sheets, and the day was dark. The pavements glinted dully, and water ran down the gutters like miniature rivers. Mrs Takamoto ignored the weather completely and set off with a determined step that had Sachiko hurrying to catch up. Within moments they reached the local shop and the muted tinkle of the bell brought the proprietor from the back room.

'Ah – Mrs Takamoto! A pleasure! What can I do for you this afternoon?'

'Just some miso and greens for the evening meal. This is Sachiko – she's recently moved into our block, and is looking for a part-time job locally. Is there a paper that has positions like that advertised?'

'Oh, I think the thing to do is look on the Internet nowadays for that kind of stuff. My son looks at some Tokyo jobs site for work – he didn't do so well in his exams, so he didn't get into college. Now he's living at home and has been doing a few odd jobs here and there. I think that's where he finds them. He's upstairs now, on the computer as usual – not doing anything useful of course! Just a minute – I'll go and ask him to come down.'

Mrs Takamoto, seeing that Sachiko was fine for the moment, picked up her umbrella and her purchases and made her farewells. 'See you later, Sachiko – I hope you have luck in your job search!'

'Thanks, Mrs Takamoto. I'll let you know how I get on when I get back.'

As Mrs Takamoto went back out into the rain, the shopkeeper reappeared with a slouching youth dressed in the latest fashion. Baggy trousers gathered at his ankles, heavy tattoos covered his arms and his hair was gelled and spiked manga style. He was happy to help though, and had soon written down a list of web addresses where he assured Sachiko she'd quickly find casual work. His attitude suggested that he himself did just enough work to get by and wasn't in a hurry to leave the parental nest. Sachiko found herself wondering what it would have been like if Tashi had grown up into such a boy. She'd never know now of course. Once again she felt the misery that was a constant nagging backdrop to her days threaten to well up in her throat. She hadn't felt complete since the moment that she realised her child was missing – a new emptiness, in a space she hadn't even realised had been filled. It was not the time or the place now. She quelled the rising tears with an effort of will, and made herself thank the young man. 'I should be able to go on the Internet at the bookshop later, and I'll check these out.'

'Don't you have a *keitei*?' he asked, incredulously.

'No, I lost my phone and haven't got around to replacing it. There wasn't really anyone that I needed to talk to.'

'Well, you'll need one if you're going to get this kind of work. They call you when they need you – so they have to be able to get hold of you fast.'

'You're right – I should have thought of that.' Sachiko felt a hot flush suffuse her cheeks. 'I suppose I'd better make that my next task.'

'You sure should. You'll be able to get one cheaply enough at any phone shop. *Ganbatte!*'

With that he was gone, back upstairs to rejoin what she thought must be, to him, the real world. Sachiko thanked the owner of the shop, and headed back into the downpour to go and buy a mobile.

I'm floating unhinged in a once-solid world. I feel like a swimmer, buffeted by great rollers that sweep over me, engulf me, and then recede, leaving me winded. From time to time I am cast upon the shore, and awake, gasping like a beached fish. Tashi is merciless. Sometimes for hours he replays the same short clip, and I see myself, see that moment looping until the person in the clip is a stranger, and I start to wonder why he is crouched down, rocking – and why, every time, he springs up and strides towards the child in the bouncer. His face is contorted. His hands reach out, grasping. And then the clip starts again, after the briefest pause on the final frame. Rewind. Play again. Rewind. Play again. It is relentless. Over every surface, the same clip, projected, offset, so that different frames are superimposed on each other. And I thought this place was a refuge? Try as I might I can't become inured to the images. I black out. Then, strangely, food is before me. I fall upon it like a starving man. How many 'me's are there? Is there a me that's sane, that is quietly living here? I reach for my notebook, to see if there's evidence of those other Harrys, but everything goes sideways. He's playing with my memories, looking at them through my eyes. Sometimes the clips are silent. At other times the sound plays too, like I'm in a high-tech cinema – the kind with quadrophonic audio. Tilt shift. It's playing inside my head. I feel him in my thoughts, probing.

'Have you got everything packed?'

'I think so. Who would have thought you could fit so much into a tiny apartment? All the things we own together!'

All around us boxes were stacked neatly, and labelled in Sachiko's careful hand: kitchen; bathroom; bedroom; storage (Harry); storage (Sachiko). Some of our belongings didn't fit into boxes and these had been sandwiched between the boxes, ready to be transported by the moving company who would be arriving shortly. Sachiko had assembled a camping kit so that we could at least make tea (and coffee for me, who had never lost the habit) and prepare some food when we arrived at the new apartment. More than 400 miles away from Tokyo – and a world away from what either of us had experienced before.

'I'm going downstairs to say some final goodbyes,' Sachiko said quietly, breaking into my thoughts. *'Call me when the movers arrive.'*

'Of course,' I replied. *'I'm going to do a last sweep of the apartment just in case we've missed something.'* I had to admit that seemed unlikely. Pale patches on the walls showed where our few pictures had once hung and the windows were bare of blinds and curtains. I watched my by-now heavily pregnant wife manoeuvre her bulk around the boxes and furniture that blocked the way. Apart from the ever-growing bulge, Sachiko appeared to have lost weight during her pregnancy – her arms and legs seemed sticklike in comparison to the mound that was to be our child, and her cheekbones were more prominent than I remembered them. She looked paler than usual too. I knew that in part this was due to savage bouts of morning sickness that had plagued her long beyond the usual three to four months, but now I wondered if there might be something else as well. She seemed more withdrawn than the old Sachiko, and more reserved. There was nothing specific I could put my finger on but she seemed different. It was ironic. We were moving north to start a new life together – away from Tokyo, which had become intolerable to Sachiko and where I felt myself trapped in a dead-end teaching job. It should have brought us closer together. But where once I had felt I could almost read her mind, now I frequently found myself asking what she was thinking, only for the shutters to drop across her eyes. *'Nothing special,'* was the invariable reply.

I put my doubts out of my mind. There was a lot more for me to deal with today. The buzzer for our flat rang, and I heard a tinny voice issuing from the intercom. I pressed the button and let the movers in.

Armed with a new phone it didn't take Sachiko long to land a job. She spotted an ad for a job as a cleaner at a local elementary school. The hours looked good, although the pay was small. But then she didn't need much.

The interview was brief – they hadn't had too many applicants so were more than happy to have a nice lady like Sachiko doing the job. There was sympathy for what she'd had to endure. Sachiko tolerated the pity. She wanted the work.

The job was menial, and meant that Sachiko would have to get up at 4.30am – but she would be finished each weekday at noon and have the afternoons and evenings free. The pay would cover her rent, but not much more.

On the way back, she popped into a sweet shop to buy a gift for Mrs Takamoto. From amongst the array of sweet, delicately perfumed and perfectly formed *wagashi* she chose several filled with sweet bean curd and coloured like shells. Sachiko walked the rest of the way home slowly, careful to avoid damaging the fragile confections.

Mrs Takamoto was of course delighted with the cakes, and instantly invited Sachiko in for tea. It seemed very right to be one of two women sitting and talking about the ways of the world, and, even though she hadn't started her new job, and it would be hard work, of a kind she wasn't used to, Sachiko felt that at least she'd made a start at a life here.

A news programme was playing on the TV that seemed to be always on in the corner. The story concerned the case of a woman who had smothered her two-year-old daughter some days before.

Mrs. Takamoto sipped her tea and pointed at the set.

'It's so sad when something like this happens. She tried to kill herself afterwards. Apparently the poor thing couldn't remember what she had done, and when she found her child dead she was broken-hearted. Why was there no one to help her? Worse, it seems like almost every week there's a case like this, where a young parent has committed *mabiki*. It's a big problem.'

Sachiko tried to think of some comment to make. She felt numb with so much death, and tended to avoid watching the news. It seemed like it never held anything positive. Seeing her at a loss for words, Mrs Takamoto hurried to correct herself.

'I'm sorry, Sachiko. It's very insensitive of me to talk like this, with everything you've been through. I bet you were a wonderful mother.'

'I wasn't. Maybe I can understand too well what drove a woman to an action such as that.'

'What do you mean?'

'After Tashi was born I went away for a while. I didn't actually go anywhere, but I stopped reacting to the things around me. To the people around me. It was like they were dead, or I was dead. Anyway, ordinary life seemed to be happening on a different plane to me; it wasn't important. That was before the tsunami. And afterwards, when I found out I was still alive, and my family were missing, it was too late. I had rejoined the human race, but I lost Tashi. Maybe in a way I killed him just as surely as the woman who smothered her baby? Maybe if I hadn't been lost in myself we would all have got out alive?'

Sachiko wondered if she'd gone too far. People didn't talk about this kind of thing, and, although Mrs Takamoto was kind, Sachiko worried that she would be shocked at any admission of mental instability. But Mrs Takamoto had her own demons.

'You mustn't think about that. Isn't there enough pain and guilt in the world without you creating more for yourself? Believe me, I know what I'm talking about. Things are bad now, but after the war they were much worse. We were a country under occupation. Child murder was a lot more common. I could tell you stories that would make your hair curl. Before they legalised abortion a lot of supposed "stillbirths" were nothing of the sort.'

Behind Mrs Takamoto was a glass case containing several wooden dolls. They were colourful and cute, each with its own expression, but Sachiko had heard rumours of a darker purpose. Some said that these *kokeshi* or 'erased children' represented the spirits of dead infants, doomed to remain in limbo as long as their mothers wept in sorrow for them. Mrs Takamoto noticed Sachiko looking at them.

'You see, even these *kokeshi* prove that what I'm saying is true. It's not a new phenomenon. In those days it was no shame for a midwife to smother a child by placing damp paper over their nose and mouth. The mother would be given a doll and told to get on with it. What else could they do? They wanted to make the best life they could for the children that survived.

'I don't think you're anything like this woman, poor thing. You didn't kill your son. The tsunami did. Sometimes it's hard to learn to let go of the past, but we have to try; we have to lay those ghosts to rest.'

Sachiko could not take her eyes off the *kokeshi*. They made her feel uneasy in a way she couldn't quite put her finger on – like a trigger for a memory – as though she had lost something important, but couldn't remember what it was.

二四

I am dragged out of sleep by the sound of screaming; a panic-inducing cry that shreds my nerves like steel wire, like nails scraping down the blackboard of my soul. I lie motionless, hoping that Sachiko will get up this time. I know there's a bottle in the warmer, but our small strategies seem useless in the face of this assault. The bedroom clock says 4.10am. The dead hour. He screams and screams. Beside me Sachiko is rigid, her breathing shallow. We are both waiting. For him to stop crying, or me to get up? I know he won't stop so it's me or her. I whisper, to break the silent deadlock, 'Sachiko! He's crying! Are you going to get up?'

Still no response. I consider poking her, but roll over instead and switch on the light.

Tashi is lying on his back, his face red, bawling. How can someone so small make so much noise? I look over at Sachiko. She's lying with her eyes open, apparently gazing at the ceiling, her face registering no particular emotion — like a sleepwalker in stasis.

I get up and cross over to the cot, whilst running through the mental checklist: nappy, feed, wind. I pick up Tashi, and bring him up close for a sniff. Nappy smells clean. I pick up his blanket and swaddle him. Sometimes this works, but now his cries redouble; it sounds like he's in agony. I transfer him to my chest, wrap a protective arm around him, then pat his back to try to calm him. It rarely works, and doesn't now. He holds himself rigid, and, instead of nestling into me, arches his back, still screaming, so that I have to shift my grip so as not to drop him. Does he need a feed? We go through into the living area.

There's a warm bottle of milk in the heater — maybe he'll take some and give me a respite from the crying, however momentary. I don't know how Sachiko can ignore it. I'm well practised by now at operating with one hand. I flip the top off, and shift Tashi into feeding position. His eyes are closed, his mouth wide open so that I can see his toothless gums, his small lapping tongue tucked back now the better to open his vocal cords. Seizing my

113

opportunity, I slip the teat of the bottle between his lips, my finger guiding it.

At once he clamps down on the teat, and my fingers too, the bony gums surprisingly strong, so that I almost drop the bottle. But he's not suckling, just holding on. At least the crying has stopped for now.

All of a sudden his eyes open, and stare straight up at me, shockingly blue. They don't seem to be the eyes of a baby at all. They look at me, measuring. I can't help feeling I've been found wanting. He seems calmer for now. I wonder if I dare risk changing him; I decide not to, and opt for putting him back in the cot again. Still he stares up at me with those disconcerting eyes, as if some other being is looking out from behind them. It makes my skin crawl – an uncomfortable reminder of those old Japanese stories about ghosts and changelings, the invisible army of the dead that surround us, always searching for a way to return to life. I've read too many of those stories, maybe, researching the book, and started imagining things that aren't there. How can I feel this way about my own son? It's like I can't feel. Like I've got no room in my heart for anyone else. Is there something monstrous in me, that I can't admit? Why am I projecting this onto poor Tashi, as if ghosts and changelings are real, and it's not just that I'm an awful father? It's not like I've had the perfect model to follow. The youngest of four, with precious little left over for me; I've always had to create myself. So I tried to create a father for him. There's a glimmering of that love I felt for him when he was first born; the wonder that such a perfect creature could have been created, even partly, by me. I can't sustain it. There's something inhuman in his eyes – something disquieting.

I crawl back into bed, glancing at the clock. Not so bad – only half an hour, but I know that there's no way I'll be able to go back to sleep before it's time to get up again. Beside me, Sachiko hasn't stirred at all. She's not sleeping either, but I know I won't get any response. I sigh and close my eyes, just as the crying starts up again...

二五

The new job was a big change for Sachiko – it was the first time she had done manual work, but she found the act of cleaning meditative and it left her mind free. She thought about the books that Hiromichi had shared with her, and started creating stories in her head as she polished floors and furniture, cleaned bathrooms, and cleared the rubbish from empty classrooms. Some of the stories were about her and Harry, alternate realities where there'd been no tsunami, or no child, or no black fog of depression sealing her away from those closest to her. At other times she changed the characters and created completely fictional environments, peopled by characters she'd never met. There was something liberating in playing out narratives that she had no emotional investment in, where the correct outcome was as clear as black and white. At times she felt guilty, as if all the stories that she created were a displacement activity, and escape from the responsibility that she should always bear, for the loss of her family. Those were bad days, but they gradually became fewer.

Her work was physically demanding, and over time she could feel herself getting stronger. There wasn't much of her pay packet left by the time she had covered her tax, rent and food, but she had grown accustomed to surviving on a tight budget so she was comfortable with that. She had little temptation to travel into the city and spend money there. Her days fell into a pleasant pattern.

She still kept an eye on news from Taro, and Fukushima prefecture. The station personnel were still working to stabilise the core and there was a general fear in Tokyo about nuclear fallout and radiation. She accepted that she, like everyone else, was probably contaminated.

All other nuclear power stations were being taken offline and power saving measures became commonplace. Everywhere were handwritten notices, 'Did you remember to switch the lights off?' The summer started to swelter, but people avoided turning on air conditioning units. Sachiko saw salarymen coming from work in short-sleeved shirts, jackets slung casually over their backs.

A different sentiment powered the city, reflected in the country at large. Community in the face of adversity. Solidarity. Up north the clean-up operation entered a second phase – most of the debris had been collected, but waited in giant piles for somewhere to be found to store it. No one was eager to take responsibility for the many tons of potentially hazardous material. Cleared of the mud and debris, the remnants of towns and cities had become bare plains scoured of life. Only the outline of foundations hinted that there were once neat houses and offices there. On higher land, prefab buildings went up as temporary housing for the displaced.

It had been many weeks now since the tsunami, and Harry and Tashi were still listed amongst the missing. Sachiko was slowly coming to terms with her loss. She had accepted that by now they were almost certainly dead. She thought she should probably try to contact Harry's family in England, although he had always been secretive about them. No one had ever come to visit Harry in Japan. There had never been a single Christmas card. She thought Harry had probably written to some family member when they got married, or when Tashi was born, but couldn't be sure. She didn't even know if both his parents were alive, or anything about his siblings. It seemed strange that they had never discussed these things. What had they talked about?

She tried to fit herself inside him, to explore the spaces in his head, but she found it harder and harder to visualise him. It all seemed so long ago. Who was this stranger that she had lived with for a decade?

She decided to start by trying to reconstruct some of their moments together. Quiet evenings. Harry had complained when she put the television on, saying it interrupted his flow of thought – similarly music. Sachiko had consequently spent quite a lot of time reading – sometimes looking over the top of her book to see him frowning whilst chewing a lock of his hair. Sometimes the keys of his laptop would hammer, and she would look over to see him absorbed. These were good times. At other times he would suffer blocks and she knew that fits of rage would soon follow.

Now that she had a phone she didn't need to use the Internet terminal any more, but she regularly dropped in to see Hiromichi. She had started writing up the stories that she created in her head in the hours she spent cleaning the school. The action of writing, of creating controlled environments and narratives for her characters, was therapeutic, and Hiromichi encouraged her, reading through the pieces that she sent him and working through them with her. In those chats with Hiromichi, Sachiko felt herself opening up more than she had ever been able to since the early days with Harry. They started to swap ideas in between their meetings by text. The messages were short and discursive, like a continuing conversation; a pithy dialogue constrained by a tiny keyboard – but they created a connection with him in a way that talking in person never did. There was always a formality between them when they were face to face.

Sachiko popped into the bookshop after work that day to pick up a new short story collection that had just come in.

'Hello, Hiromichi-san – I thought I'd come by and get a copy of that new Yoshimoto collection – the one you mentioned yesterday. Has it come in yet?'

'Hello, Sachiko-san. It did, right on time – lovely edition too.' He held up a typically pocket-sized book, still in its dustcover.

'Do you have time for a cup of tea or are you rushing off? The shop is quiet this time of day. I'd love to chat more about the story you left me yesterday.'

'Sure,' replied Sachiko with a smile. 'It was just a quick piece. I'm sure that there's plenty wrong with it – but I'm very happy you found it interesting enough to want to chat with me about it.'

'I found it a thought-provoking subject. It's not often that modern writers bother to think about the old stories any more. We're too interested in picking up Western myths, and Western writers, to remember those old stories about changelings and ghosts. And the way you described the mountains, it really made my skin crawl. What inspired you?'

'It was that story that I read the day I came into the bookshop for the first time. It really seemed to speak to me – and the way that the characters in it spoke and acted towards each other reminded me of how it was with Harry.'

They were both silent for a few moments. Sachiko was lost in memory, and Hiromichi didn't know how to comment on her reminiscence of her husband without it seeming inappropriate, or disrespectful. He had gleaned that her husband and child had been lost in the tsunami, but sensed too that the story was more complex than that.

Sachiko cleared her throat, nervously, and went on, embarrassed that she had gone too far.

'I'm sorry – it's not your problem of course. Relationships are never perfect. I shouldn't have said anything. Look, I've just remembered that I need to pick something up from the laundry before it closes. How much is it for the Yoshimoto?'

Hiromichi was hurt that she had resumed the formal tone. He kept his voice neutral whilst he named the price, and wrapped the book for her as she searched in her purse for the right money.

'Thanks – I'll see you soon.'

There was just a hint of artificiality in her voice, and she didn't meet his eyes as she left. Hiromichi felt his heart sink, but of course it could be no other way. Her family had not even been confirmed dead, and there was much he didn't know about her.

Sachiko kept her back straight as she left the shop – but in fact she felt as though a heavy weight was on her shoulders. She felt confused. She'd been able to lose herself in books, been able to ignore the change in her relationship with Hiromichi, but every so often reality would intrude, and she would remember she was freshly bereaved, and feel that she had to put that distance back between them. She could tell she had hurt Hiromichi, but what could she do? She barely noticed the short walk back to Mrs Takamoto's from the bookshop. Her eyes were full of tears. It had been his expression that had undone her – behind that gentle concern was a need, a desire even, that she wasn't ready to deal with. It brought back that feeling of being trapped – like the caged bird in the story. She couldn't remember what the story was called, but she remembered the caged bird that was unhappy in its prison, yet too terrified to fly free. Her tears were falling freely now. She wiped them away, but more came.

She turned the corner into her street. As she approached the block she could see Mrs Takamoto outside, sweeping the front steps. She paused a moment, tried to stop the tears, dabbing at them with a cloth, surreptitiously, but it was no use. Mrs Takamoto had spotted her, and Sachiko knew her posture would give her away.

'Sachiko, Sachiko!' Mrs Takamoto called to her as she approached. 'Sachiko – is everything ok?'

Sachiko felt ashamed. As the distance between them narrowed it felt as though her feet were mired in sand. She wanted to stop, to turn away; not to be an object of pity; a woman who couldn't cope; that cried and showed her feelings.

Now Mrs Takamoto was coming towards her.

'Dear Sachiko – what is it? Why don't you answer me?'

'I'm sorry, Mrs Takamoto – so sorry. It's nothing.'

She fought to get her voice past the lump in her gullet. It hurt to speak, as though her misery had locked the muscles in her throat into a tight knot, and she couldn't quite force her feelings past it, or open her voice box enough to emit words.

'Well, it doesn't seem like nothing. Come on now – Father's out and he won't be back for a while. Why don't you come in and have a nice cup of tea? It will make you feel much better – I'm sure of it. And we can have a good chat about what's wrong, *ne*?'

Mrs Takamoto grabbed Sachiko's elbow with surprising strength and steered her towards the door, and through to the flat. Sachiko let herself be guided and seated in the parlour. As Mrs Takamoto bustled away to make tea, Sachiko settled herself into the overstuffed sofa. She had stopped sobbing now, but her chest still felt tight with misery, and she couldn't draw a full breath. What had broken the dam back there? One minute they'd been happily discussing literature, and the next the conversation had switched to another level entirely. Of course. She cursed herself for mentioning Harry.

Mrs Takamoto came back with a tray, and Sachiko scrambled to her feet to help her.

'Sit down, Sachiko – I think I can manage a tea tray, even at my advanced age.'

Sachiko watched as she poured two cups of fragrant tea, and bowed her head in thanks as Mrs Takamoto passed one to her. She nestled it between her hands, blowing away the steam that rose from its surface. She gazed down into the depths of the cup, where a few flakes of tea had settled on the bottom. She could almost trust herself to speak now. She blew gently, and then took a sip of the scalding tea.

Next to her she felt Mrs Takamoto's bulk settle onto the sofa. She raised her head.

'Thank you so much, Mrs Takamoto. I'm so sorry to intrude, and to be so much trouble to you. I don't know what came over me. I feel much better now.'

'Are you sure, dear?'

Mrs Takamoto fixed her with a familiar gaze – the one that saw right through her.

'Yes, really, Mrs Takamoto. I suppose, sometimes I remember, and it all feels like it's too much.'

'It's just that you seemed perfectly happy when you left here earlier. You were humming in fact. I commented on it to Father as you went past. I said, "Listen to how happy she is, Shinji – like a woman going to meet someone who brings her joy" – or at least a woman looking forward to something, hmm?'

Sachiko gazed down into her lap, and watched her fingers twisting the cloth, still damp from her tears.

'I went to the bookshop.' She didn't look up. There was a sense of shame now, mixed in with the misery.

'Well, of course. Reading has been such a comfort to you. And all the writing you've been doing too. But what's upset you so much eh? Was it something you read? Have you had some bad news?'

'No news – I've still heard nothing about them. I don't suppose I ever will now. No – it's not that. It's hard to explain. I'm not quite sure I understand myself what's set me off. I'll be alright, I promise.'

She looked up and held Mrs Takamoto's gaze. And it was true, as she sat there, sipping tea, she could feel her control coming back. It was Hiromichi that had upset her – and was it because she could feel him getting too close?

'You are allowed to have a life you know. It's been so hard for you all this time, in limbo. Not allowing yourself to move on. Is that what's worrying you? It's a natural reaction – I think women have been feeling this way forever. The men leave and we have to pick up the pieces and move on.'

'But Harry didn't leave. He was taken from me.'

'And how was it before? Before the tsunami? Forgive me for being so blunt, but I formed the impression that things might have been a little stressful. Were you happy together, Sachiko?'

'I suppose not all the time. I found it hard, the last couple of years at least. We argued sometimes, but the other times, when we didn't argue, they were worse.'

'What married couple doesn't have their problems? You don't always argue, but you feel it inside. Father and I, we've had some times.'

Sachiko thought of the way they were together. The gentle impatience.

'You obviously love each other very much though?'

'Yes we do, but don't imagine everything has always been perfect. We're old now, and so used to each other neither of us could imagine being with anyone else – but he wasn't always so faithful, you can be sure.'

Sachiko was shocked at her openness, and it must have shown in her face because Mrs Takamoto chuckled.

'You didn't expect that did you? Well, there's no point in us keeping secrets from each other. We're both women – if we can't be honest with each other, what is the world coming to, eh?'

She looked expectantly at Sachiko, and Sachiko realised it was time to come clean – as much with herself as with Mrs Takamoto.

'You're right. We do need to be honest with each other – and I need to be honest with myself. It's Mr Hiromichi, who runs the bookshop. I realised that I'm... starting to have some feelings for him – and it was a big shock for me. It made me feel terrible.'

Mrs Takamoto reached out and gave Sachiko's shoulder a comforting squeeze.

'It's only natural, dear. Just like I said before. The men have always gone away, and it's left to the women to continue. Your body's only doing what it's designed to do. You're too young to spend the rest of your life alone. And I know Mr Hiromichi – he's a lovely man. You have nothing to fear from him.'

She leaned forward and took both of Sachiko's hands in hers, so Sachiko was forced to look into her eyes.

'You have nothing – nothing – to feel guilty about. You understand?'

'I'm sorry, Mrs Takamoto – that's just what you haven't understood. It's not guilt I feel – it's fear. I'm afraid of getting trapped – just when I'm learning to be free.'

'He's not the kind that would be controlling, Sachiko – I'm sure he'll let you take things at your own pace. Now dry your tears, young lady. You'll be fine.'

Sachiko dabbed at her eyes with the cloth, whilst Mrs Takamoto watched her, speculatively.

'Why don't you stay away tomorrow? I could do with some help, and a little break won't do things any harm. And when you've decided how you feel, he can do things the old fashioned way, and take you out for the evening.'

'But that's just the thing – he hasn't said anything. It's just a feeling I had.'

'A woman's feelings are never wrong, my dear. Maybe you're not quite ready to feel that way about someone yet – or maybe it's what you need. You've been through a lot. Would you like some more tea?'

'You've been so kind, Mrs Takamoto. I've had plenty of tea now – thank you. I'll think about what you have said.'

'You do that. And don't forget – if you want to understand your feelings give yourself a little distance from them. You might be able to see what's going on then. Oh and one other thing – I really could do with your help tomorrow. The couple with the baby are moving out of number 12, and I could do with a hand to turn it out.'

'Of course. What time?'

'Is 4.30pm ok for you?'

'That's fine. I'll be finished work long before then. And thanks again, Mrs Takamoto. It's wonderful how you make everything seem clearer.'

'Old age does that for you, I find. Nothing seems quite so upsetting any more. See you tomorrow!'

Sachiko climbed the stairs to her room. She did feel better – at least not so frightened and miserable any more. And she felt lighter too – the hard twist had gone from her throat, and, almost, she felt like singing, which was odd, because she had a voice like a bullfrog. She opened the door and felt the joy of coming home to her own space where everything was just as she had left it. She closed the door behind her and sank down on the matting. There was just one thing to do. Today was Tuesday and she had a day off on Friday. That left Thursday evening clear. She pulled out her phone and composed a quick message for Hiromichi.

'Sorry I had to rush off. Can we meet on Thursday evening? It would be good to chat.'

二六

Sometimes the dreams come, not in the form of memories, but as visions. I find myself in a town that appears to be abandoned. The streets are deserted, and the shops not so much shut up, as temporarily closed and not returned to. Looking through the windows I can see a thin layer of dust on the surfaces inside and on merchandise in the windows. There are few cars in the streets; bicycles left as if their owners are about to return – one sturdy *mamachari* even has shopping in the rear basket, now rotted down to an indistinguishable black mess.

Still no sign of any people, and an eerie quiet lies over all, almost like a blanket of silence. Beneath my feet, weeds and grasses push up through the cracks in the pavement, with the brute intransigence of vegetable life.

I walk up to the first house and try the door. Unlocked, it opens easily at my touch, and I step inside. In the dim light from the half-shuttered window I witness a scene of sudden abandonment. Breakfast half-eaten, dirty dishes in the sink – and still no people. It looks like a family lived here, and they left quickly. A faded area on the wall suggests a picture might have hung there recently. And, over everything, that thin layer of dust. What happened in this place?

I climb the stairs to the upper floor. Here too is disarray; futons still out; discarded nightclothes. I go back downstairs and step outside. The ubiquitous vending machines, still powered, offer a selection of chilled beverages. I am not surprised to find them functional. From the depths of the ocean to the lonely peak of Mount Fuji, vending machines march over the land supplying every necessity of life. I shake my head, to clear it, feel my feet on the ground, touch myself. It has to be a dream, but it seems too tangible. Is Tashi showing me this place? I close my eyes – but when I open them again I'm still here. Can this place be real?

I wander back through the village. Here is the post office, and next to it the police station. Like all the other buildings they are empty of people – but as I approach I can see that notices have been taped to the door. I try to puzzle out the characters. There is a date – five days after the tsunami – and the symbol for radiation. Is this a vision of the past, or the future? The radiation... I remember Tashi's news reports – his gleeful recounting of the worsening situation at the Fukushima nuclear power plant. Perhaps this village is close to there, and had been evacuated as a precaution. Judging from the dust it seems like the inhabitants have been gone for some time. I wonder what has become of them now. Why is Tashi showing me this? I have to assume it's something to do with him.

'Good question, Pops – after all it's not as though you give a damn about all these people – to you they're just "Japanese" – you assume they'll deal with it just like everything else. What place could there be for you in a country of a million displaced? What do you care what happened to any of them? What's become of my mother? She's gone where everyone else went – first to the refugee centres, and then to the cities, if they had the money or any connections; temporary housing if they had none. A one-way diaspora. They'll probably never be able to return to their old lives. Do you like it here? The radiation can't affect us of course. I'm getting very bored of that dreary old shack.'

I don't know what to say. What can I say? I stare at him mutely and think of the millions of lives changed forever on one fateful day. And if I had gone back, would it have made any difference?

I wake from fitful sleep full of dreams that are a confusing mix of events remembered and constructed, a fragmented narrative that mirrors the surrealism of my waking hours. The first thing that goes through my head is, prosaically, that I need a piss. I've gone beyond hunger and everything is overlaid with a kind of febrile aura. I stretch and realise that everything hurts. It's as if I've been climbing mountains all night, instead of spending uncounted days and nights watching Tashi's newsreels. I open the door and go outside. Looking up I can't see the sun through the grey clouds that blanket the sky; I have no idea what time of day it is. The forest is quiet.

The trees loom tall above me, and between their branches I can see metre-wide spider webs glinting – each with their black, red and yellow guardian squatting in the centre. I'm not afraid of spiders, but these give a painful (if not fatal) bite if disturbed. It had seemed like a grand adventure, hiding myself in the forest, getting away from everything to rediscover my inner muse, but now I understand that my plan of running into the mountains and hiding myself away may have been overly romantic. I lack the ability to survive in this inhospitable land. I wonder how much longer I can endure this, and whether I should stop lying to myself and face up to what I left behind.

I feel that now familiar sensation of cold fingers on the back of my neck, and the hairs all over my body stand up.

'Let me refresh your memory, Papa... that is if you feel you can trust me?'

'Tashi!'

'Yes I'm back. Had a couple of things to take care of on the other side, but it's all sorted out now. Did you miss me, Papa?'

'Is it really you? Why do you keep coming back here like this to torture me? Wasn't losing you and your mother enough punishment for me?'

'You'd think so. Even now you can't accept you did anything wrong. The fact is in the teeth of the earthquake you ran away like the coward you are. And that wasn't even the worst of the things you did. You could have stopped to help them – the neighbours who had taken you in and accepted you into their community, and the wife who had given up everything so that you could pursue your dream of writing. But you didn't, did you?'

'How could I help her? She'd stopped talking to me weeks before. You know that. It wasn't my fault – it was yours! She was fine before you were born. We both were.'

'That's not true, is it, Papa? You know it isn't... all those silences... that bloodless war. It hasn't been fine for a long time now. Even before you left Tokyo it had started to go wrong. How could you think that having a child would fix the cracks in your relationship? You were never fit to be a father.'

'I wanted to be one. I was really looking forward to it. But you were never an easy baby. From the moment you were born you screamed and cried. It was as though you didn't want to be here in the first place. You literally drove me insane!'

'You're right. I didn't. Babies are born with precognition you know. I knew what was going to happen, and I wasn't happy about it. But there was nothing I could do to prevent it. That's why I cried. I knew what she would do, my mother, I knew she would retreat into that cocoon of silence – that she was a coward. And I knew that you would both take the easy way out. You were both responsible for my death. So convenient that the tsunami came along when it did. Even now you could go back. It might take a little explaining, why you walked out leaving your family to certain destruction, but you'd probably get away with it. Especially being a foreigner, and therefore unpredictable. You and I are both still listed as officially "missing pre-sumed dead" you know.'

'And what now? How is it working out for you, lost in the moun-tains bereft of all human company... is that what you wanted? Just how is that book going anyway? Met any ghosts lately?'

There were two Tashis warring, in my head, amidst the memories and fantasies that kept surfacing, drowning out the present. There was our baby Tashi, and the memories of making him, and being with Sachiko, and our life together, and our hopes for each other; and then there was this mocking creature – this ghost, this manifestation, this changeling. This was not our child – this being that was too knowing, and too knowledgeable. If only I could understand. If only I knew why he was here.

We had a child. This much I know – we had a child, and it feels like I've been reliving those days. How could I have forgotten, those last weeks, what it was like to be a father?

Remembering what it was like when he was born. She needed an emergency caesarian. There was nothing I could do to help her – it was like she'd gone to another place, there was so much pain. She barely made any noise but it was in her eyes, like dark bruises in a face too pale. As soon as she went into labour it was like life had switched to a different rhythm, fallen out of time. Days and nights blurred beneath the strip lights of the hospital corridor. I waited, and tried to distract myself by reading, still researching the myths book. Already starting to ask myself how those myths were born; what dark currents of the inexplicable had caused people to try to describe them in the first place – the children stolen, switched, replaced. Where was the grain of truth that had created the myth, that sandy excrescence that gradually rarefied into a pearl of great price?

It was impossible to cross-reference. In those days many children were killed at birth – life was too much of a gamble to stack the odds against the children still living. Amidst so much child mortality, who was to say if some had been killed for other reasons? Was it because they were different, alien, because their eyes were too knowing?

And was that why I'd not been able to connect with Tashi? My thoughts jumbled. I tried to sort out the memories but it was as if those fresh visions of the day before were blurring the lines I thought I knew, the reality I had believed was true.

Perhaps Tashi was right: I needed to stop running away. Perhaps I owe that to Sachiko after all. I no longer know what is true or false; how can I believe the claims of a ghost, who could be purely the product of my imagination – a manifestation of my guilt? He claims she is alive and has moved to the city. But he also claims that I killed him, that she killed him – that he didn't die in the tsunami after all. I think back to the moments before I left; the empty baby carrier hanging on the wall; the lack of Tashi. How can I know what is true? How can I sort out the real memories? How can I become sane again?

Abruptly a pain like I had never known filled my head and burned in my limbs. It was as though someone had replaced all my blood with fire. I clung to consciousness, feeling earth and stones clenched beneath my fingers as I clawed at the earth in agony, hearing many voices through the static that filled my head – shouting, laughing, screaming, cheering, a babel of voices raised in argument, exultation, song. And those eyes: those eyes bored into my soul, and there was no respite.

They meet at a tiny local *izakaya* – the kind with six seats along a narrow counter. The wood is old and pitted, and the specials of the day are written out on pegs hanging on the wall.

Ashtrays jostle for space with chopsticks, soy sauce, green tea powder, toothpicks and chilli. Conversation is easy. They talk about the stories Hiromichi recommended to Sachiko – the fresh voices that come through from the more modern pieces towards the end of the collection. They talk about Taeko Kono and Banana Yoshimoto. Sachiko tells Hiromichi she's glad he's brought her to a literature where women aren't afraid to write shocking and honest things. It makes her feel like writing herself, in a way that 10 years with a frustrated writer never could. She feels free of guilt. They talk about Sachiko's writing. At first Hiromichi hadn't known what to make of it; it seemed so menacing and stark that it had made him rethink his opinion of Sachiko and want to relearn her again. But it's good to talk, working through their different ideas of each other seems to bring them closer together. Snacks and *shochu* – the easy intimacy of a meal shared from many small dishes. The warmth of conversation. Squeezed together at the counter, parts of their bodies inevitably touch. The owner teases them and keeps their glasses topped up. Empty dishes are replaced by full – *gyoza*, *yakitori* and *sashimi*. They eat and drink their fill.

It's been a long time for either of them. The conversation, so fluid, abruptly stops – replaced by a silent need. They realise they are holding hands. Hiromichi blushes, makes to let go… Sachiko stops him. *O kanjo onegaishimasu…* the bill is paid, thanks given. They stoop through the fluttering *noren* that line the doorway and break out into the night air.

'Where shall we go?'

'Why don't you come back to my place for coffee?'

'I'd love to.'

A silent promise, implicit in the touch of their hands. A short walk back through the quiet neighbourhood; the evening chilly enough to justify walking close together. Hiromichi leads Sachiko through into the dark and silent bookshop. She has never seen its night-time guise; dark corners; rows and rows of books – it feels bigger now. Hiromichi draws her forward to the counter, behind it and through a curtain. They remove their shoes. No words.

Beyond is a small room, with a divider down the middle, now open. On one side is a kitchen/study area, sink, toaster, stereo, computer – all the elements of a life for one. The other side is raised and covered with traditional tatami. An alcove at the far end houses the ancestral shrine. There is a low table and cushions.

'Sit please, Sachiko.' Hiromichi settles down beside her. They turn face-to-face, and then they are kissing, exploring chastely and then more urgently the new tastes of each other. Sachiko surprises him – at once all planes and angles interrupted by sudden softness. He lets his fingers caress the silk of her nape and feels her fingers dig into his back. There is the demand for sex, but also a need for sheer human companionship; her loneliness answered by a still small place within him. They kiss forever.

Some time later they break apart and gaze, knowing but silent, into one another's eyes. It's not the moment for words; but much has been exchanged. Hiromichi stands, crosses the room to the stereo – Hikaru Hayashi fills the air – a lyrical and meditative set of variations on a lament.

'Would you like a drink? I've only got beer.'

'Sure – that would be fine.'

'I've wanted to tell you how I feel for a while. I didn't know how… and there was the matter of your family.'

'Sssh.' Sachiko put a finger to his lips. 'We don't need to talk about that now. I've been feeling the same way about you – but it didn't seem right. It does now though. I'm not exactly sure what has changed – maybe it's just time passing. I'm starting to put some roots down here with the new job. But I think this is ok for me now. Should we talk about it so much?'

Hiromichi was thoughtful, pondering this. 'To be totally honest,

Sachiko, I haven't had a lot of experience with women. So I'm not sure what to talk about.'

'Then let's not talk – let's go to bed. Please?'

Sachiko was shocked at herself – was she moving too fast? Hiromichi didn't answer, but took her hand again and drew her to her feet. She followed him, in a daze, to a back staircase and up the steep and narrow steps to his bedroom. They untwisted buttons, sundered zips, revealed what had been imagined, all in the shadows from the papered windows. They fell together at last into the covers and charted the reaches of each other's bodies.

二八

I think I'm back in control. I can move normally again. It's dark inside the hut, but chinks of light shine through the gaps in the walls, bright enough to see my hands. Bright enough to read by. I sit up and feel for the bottle of water. I feel a dreadful thirst, tongue swollen and dry, and I am hungry – beyond hunger with the shaky panic of low blood sugar.

I rummage around the hut, looking for something to chew on and calm the pangs. I find a packet of fish, and rip into it with my teeth. It is dry and salty. I wash it down with a mouthful of stale water from my bottle. It tastes like it's been in there too long, but it helps a little bit. I go delving again for something else to eat, but find my notebook instead. Opening it, I start to leaf through the pages. I find jottings on odd Japanese words and concepts; unfamiliar kanji; many notes about Tashi's development. I see my writing become fragmented as the endless crying takes its toll. The notebook contains only hints of what I had relived again and again over those last days, reminding me what it was like to live with that constant wailing, varying only in its pitch and intensity. Notes on patterns of feeding and sleeping. Telephone numbers of movers, and the new school that I started at up north. Bus times; class times; unfamiliar vocabulary; northern dialect and sayings. A life in exile. Notes from my time here, fragmented, undated – the handwriting sloping in many directions, trailing at strange angles off the page. Amidst these are fragments of speech – fragments heard or imagined? I had started hearing voices, becoming increasingly displaced from reality. There are many references to Tashi, to the strange, hungry ghost-child that seemed to be a changeling from an ancient Japanese tale, or a *gaki*, an unquiet spirit whose death had been violent and premature. I describe the feeling of a weight on my chest when I am sleeping. I have read of rituals for placating unhappy spirits, but I do not know them.

There are lucid passages, some I remember writing. Others I don't. I try to fit myself inside those other Harrys. Were these things real or imagined? Is the ghost Tashi real, or has my fevered mind created a narrative from the extremes of psychosis?

I put the notebook down and listen to the world around me. From somewhere I hear the rush of water and a crow's 'caw caw caw'. The susurration of leaves suggests many trees; the wind soughs through them, and I can just hear the sound of crickets or cicadas. Light shines around the frame of the door, which is shut. Locked? I can't tell. Perhaps I am trapped in here.

I get up and walk towards the door. Getting up is harder than I expected, and my legs feel weak. I'm confused. How long has it been since I arrived here? I put my hand up to my face. The beard that had started to come in has grown full and bushy, and the cheekbones that it covers jut more sharply than they should. Near the door is a metal washbasin with a polished steel mirror above it. The face that gazes back at me isn't mine – or rather it is, but I've aged 20 years. My eyes were never that sunken. Deep lines groove my forehead and form vertical seams down my cheeks to a thick greying beard. The rest of me is skeletal. I have never seen myself so thin.

The door is secured with a simple wooden latch and opens easily. I don't know why I was scared about being locked in. It feels as though I have been trapped here for a long time. Opening it, I look out. Daytime. Mid-morning? I recognise the clearing, the path, the water dipper outside the lodge, but it all seems different. Then I put my finger on it. I arrived here in early spring, but now the trees around are in full leaf and that's why it feels unfamiliar – the green walls rise around me impenetrably where before I could see down the slopes to the valley below. It's an odd feeling – both comforting and a little terrifying.

I cross to where bamboo pipes feed water to a shallow stone pond, and take a long refreshing drink from the metal dipper resting there. I can feel the cold water hydrating every part of my body, and the shock of it as it travels down my throat. Close by the stream burbles and amidst the thick trees dozens of spider webs glint in the sunshine. The back half of the hut is on stilts, and the land drops away sharply on that side down to the valley below. The path that brought me here snakes down and around a bend and disappears. I know where it goes – to join the hiking track that leads to Ryusendo Cave – but I'm not ready to leave just yet. I'd like to know the date. It feels as if I've been here for weeks. Could that be possible? When did I lose all that time? The – daydreams? – hallucinations? – felt like they took moments. How am I still alive? Barely. Suddenly my legs won't hold me any more and I have to sit down. The ground is hard and stony, and I notice my nails are thick with grime; my hands look like those of a vagrant. What have I become?

I turn back to the hut. Inside all is silent and dark save for where the light from the doorway illuminates the interior. Without the flickering of images on the beams it looks long unused – abandoned even. Dust lies thick upon every surface and many spiders have made their homes amongst the beams. There should be more food squirrelled away, and I know there are several more caches hidden nearby. I hope they're still there. The only living creatures I have seen are spiders and birds. Could I eat spiders? I don't think I have come to that yet.

I find myself drifting into more memories, of Sachiko, spending *Hanami* in Tokyo – sharing sweet *sake* and giggling maniacally beneath the cherry trees, but I can't do that now. I shake my head and step outside the door again. Pausing at the stone pool I empty my bottle and refill it with the cold, sweet water. Tashi is nowhere to be seen, nor can I feel his presence – that strange density of energy that makes the hairs on the back of my neck stand up. There seems no way of explaining it unless I'm experiencing flashes of lucidity between episodes of madness. Am I mad? Or could it be that Tashi is real? I still have no way of knowing.

I can't risk going back, but if I stay here I will be lost forever.

二九

It didn't feel quite right to stay for breakfast. Sachiko thought of the many times she had prepared the morning meal for Harry – sticky rice, fermented soy beans, smoked oily fish, miso. Harry said breakfast was one of the best things about Japan, although he drew the line at raw eggs: he'd always preferred them soft-boiled.

And so she rose quietly, leaving Hiromichi still sleeping, looking younger somehow with his hair tousled and his lips slightly parted. They had held each other in the night, but at some point must have rolled apart. Now he slept like a man used to sleeping alone, carelessly, one arm flung out.

Sachiko gathered her clothes and descended the steep and narrow stairs as quietly as possible. She dressed quickly once she reached his office and slipped through the curtain into the front of the shop. The street door was locked, but the latch turned easily. She paused for a moment, wondering if leaving so quietly, without having spoken to Hiromichi, was the right thing to do. It seemed like she was sneaking away, as if she felt bad about what had happened between them. But truly she didn't. She felt as light as air. Maybe she should leave a note? But it was too early for writing; she needed tea first – and she didn't know if he was the kind of man who was grumpy in the morning. It seemed safer not to find out – to keep this happy mood intact.

She lifted the latch and slipped through the door, hearing the tinkle of the bell as she did so. Damn. Too late to go back now. She quickened her steps towards home.

It was a beautiful morning. It had rained in the night and the streets seemed freshly washed. All around her the city was slowly waking up; people hanging out futons; kids heading off to school in their neat navy and white uniforms, satchels on their backs and lunch bags swinging. Everyone seemed to be going somewhere. Sachiko turned into her street, and there were Mr and Mrs Takamoto, tending the plants outside their block. Would they be able to tell? Never mind. Sachiko walked towards them with a smile '*Ohayo, ohayo goza-imashita.*'

Mrs Takamoto was the first to reply.

'And a good morning to you too, Sachiko. You're up early today. I thought you had a day off?'

'Yes, I do – I'm not working again until Monday. It's such a lovely morning it seems a shame not to be out in it.'

Mr Takamoto chuckled.

'It's the type of day that's kind to old bones. You get to really feel the Tokyo winters when you get to my age.'

'Shush you – she doesn't want to hear about your aches and pains.'

Mrs Takamoto's indulgent tone belied her words.

'Sachiko – it seems like there's a spring in your step. The fine morning must really have put you in a good mood. Lovely weather to have a couple of days off. What will you do with yourself?'

Sachiko was nonplussed. She hadn't really planned anything past the evening with Hiromichi, and now she'd left him without even a note.

Mrs Takamoto, as usual, missed nothing.

'Well, it's a lovely day to take in a park. That's what I'd do today if I were still young. Father's knees aren't what they used to be, eh, Shinji?'

Sachiko blushed. She wondered if Mrs Takamoto had guessed exactly where she'd been, but was too polite to mention it in front of her husband.

'That's a lovely idea, Mrs Takamoto. Maybe I'll do that. I've got a couple of other things to do first though. I'll be back down later – let me know if you need any more help – I'll have plenty of time over the weekend. Bye for now.'

As Sachiko disappeared inside the building, Mrs Takamoto turned to her husband.

'Did you see the spring in her step? She told me she had been having a few problems with a young man, but, if you ask me, they're over that now. I'm glad. She deserves to be happy.'

'Oh you're such a romantic,' Mr Takamoto's tone was gruff. 'Those kinds of liaisons are just empty fun. I wouldn't read too much into it.'

'You were more romantic when we met, Shinji.'

'That was 50 years ago, my dear. We've both learned a lot since then.'

He plucked an early peony, now fading, and held it out.

'If only she knew how fast time runs out. Life fades away, just like this flower, and we end up on the dustheap. It's true, what they say – youth is wasted on the young.'

'At least the young are optimistic, Shinji. They live in the moment – and maybe, all things considered, it's better if we don't know what lies ahead. Anyway – come inside now – I'll make you some tea.'

I woke up and found myself on an empty bus, seated towards the back. For the longest time I didn't know how to react. I stared out the windows and tried to work out where I was. One or two landmarks were familiar and I realised that I must be on the road to Taro. Was this another dream? This wasn't a scene that I had lived through before. The landscape was not as I remembered it from the months when I had lived there with Sachiko. We passed great piles of debris, waiting on a more final disposal. Missing buildings; the sea wall smashed and a bare swathe of earth, with only foundations showing; no colourful gaggle of fishing boats. Up by the hospital the bus made a new stop, at some temporary housing that had been erected on the site of a car park. I could see little of what went on inside – the windows were modestly curtained, and only a few children's toys and the inevitable *mamacharis* hinted that someone lived there. The station was open – I could see a lighted train carriage outlined against the already darkening sky at the railway stop. But it didn't feel as though Taro was open for business. It had always felt like a quiet, little local place, but now it felt desolate.

I had known, in my head, that all we had shared together had been washed away in a moment – but seeing it like this was another thing altogether. I had become at least a little inured to the videos and news reports that Tashi bombarded me with daily – never knowing if they were the product of my own mind, hardly even believing them. But now a sense of utter loss struck me, piledriving me into the ground.

I needed to find out if she had survived. The need was urgent now. And there was the matter of Tashi; of what I thought I had learned about his passing. I had to find out which version was true.

Before the disaster there had been a single guest house in Taro, maintained by the village elders, and more than sufficient for the few tourists who came on fishing trips. The bus arrived at its final stop, and I got up, more from habit than anything. I didn't know how much to pay the driver. Where had I got on? The driver looked at me strangely, as I went through my pockets looking for change. After weeks in the forest this sudden return to normality was too much for me. I had been thinking in English for too long. The bus driver, seeing me struggling, said, not unkindly, '*Daijobu* – don't worry.' I nodded mutely and got off the bus.

There were a couple of people at the bus stand, chatting with their backs to me. One of them turned around, and I recognised the ticket officer from Taro station – who recognised me, at the same moment, for we'd often seen each other in the days when I commuted to my teaching job. I couldn't recall his name.

'Mr Turnbull. We thought you were dead!'

The words tumbled out in Japanese. I played catch-up whilst I sorted them out, translated them.

'But where are you going now, at this time?'

'I thought the guest house might have a room?'

'I'm so sorry, Mr Turnbull, but it was destroyed in the tsunami. Everything was. There's no one left now – everyone but us has left. I was lucky my house was above the old tsunami stone, and was spared. Mr Turnbull – we thought you had died. You are on the list of the missing. Please, can I ask, where have you been?'

As I stood there, looking at the ticket officer, wondering what to reply to his question, Tashi blinked into existence. His face was marred by a long cut and the back of his head oddly shaped, as if it had been bashed in. I looked down at myself and noticed that I appeared to be covered in fresh blood. Tashi's piercing tones rang in my ears.

'Tell them why you ran away, Papa. Tell them what happened.'

I looked around, wildly – but the ticket officer did not seem to be aware of Tashi's presence. He and the others looked at me inquiringly.

'I've been… away… in the forest. I missed everything. I went running, but then I got sick. I haven't been very well at all. I don't know what happened.'

Tashi has come closer to me now, reaching out to grasp me with his insubstantial fingers. I feel nothing – but where his hand touches bloody marks remain, like stigmata. Suddenly a line from *Macbeth* comes, inconsequentially, into my head, 'Here's the smell of blood still. All the perfumes of Arabia will not sweeten this little hand. Oh, oh, oh!' I pluck, ineffectually, at his wraithlike form, trying to push him away – then cover my ears with my hands like a child, trying to block out the sound of his voice, the people around me receding into the background.

'Leave me alone. Leave me alone. Why are you following me? Why have you brought me back here?'

His reply comes in cold and angry tones. 'I told you, Papa – it's time to pay for what you did. Did you think you could get away with it forever?'

On the periphery, several more people have arrived, dressed in the bright red uniforms of the volunteer fire corps. I feel more hands, solid ones this time, grabbing me, holding me and pulling me to my feet. Voices murmur in my ears, but I can barely hear them over Tashi's cries – the same screaming that had filled his waking hours in those weeks and months before I had left.

Then the pain in my head is back, sharp points of agony around my forehead, at the temples, and the nape of the neck, as though I am wearing a crown of thorns – the illusion so real I almost expect to feel blood dripping down my face. I am vaguely aware of screaming in agony, and their grip tightens to compensate for my writhing. They talk fast, in Japanese, obviously concerned. Someone makes a phone call. After a while another man comes – older, with capable hands and cool instruments. He checks my pulse and heart rate in a businesslike manner. I am aware of the prick of a needle. Not long after that I feel consciousness fade.

Part 3

'The nail that sticks out gets hammered in.'
Japanese proverb

I opened my eyes and found myself in a hospital bed. I squeezed them shut and opened them again, several times. The room grew steady, but my head was still thick as cotton – as though I had been heavily sedated for days. I wondered how long I had been out. I tried to move my arm, only to realise that it was connected, via a bandage around my bicep, to a drip that stood beside the bed. A monitor behind recorded my pulse with regular beeps.

Looking around I could see that I was in a single-bed room, and that the open door looked out onto a corridor that was empty at the moment. To my right was a window covered with a slatted blind, through which sunlight cast bars of light onto the bed. Carefully, for I didn't want to disturb the tubes that fed into my arm, I sat up, and, when the waves of dizziness and nausea subsided, swung around until I was seated on the edge of the bed with my feet on the ground. On the monitor my heart rate speeded up – lines racing frantically across the screen – and I listened to see if the increased activity would bring anyone running. There was nothing to disturb the silence. I clenched my fists, rolled my head experimentally on my neck, then flexed my shoulders and ankles. I felt weak, but apart from that everything seemed to be in working order.

I stood up and took one step towards the window, only to be brought up short by the pipework. I didn't really want to remove anything without knowing what I was doing, but luckily the monitor cable was long, and the drip stand was on wheels. Another step brought me to the window.

My room seemed to be on the ground floor. I looked out onto a car park, and, beyond that, an unfamiliar street. I was fairly sure I wasn't in Taro any more. Was this yet another lucid dream?

Then from behind me I heard a soft voice.

'Mr Turnbull, Sir, you should not be out of bed!'

I looked around. At the door was a young woman, neatly dressed in a nurse's uniform. I didn't recognise her any more than the street outside, suggesting I had either imagined arriving in Taro, or I had been brought here when I was unconscious.

'Where am I?'

'You're in a hospital in Miyako. And you really ought to stay in bed until Doctor-san says it's alright for you to be up.'

Crossing the room she took my arm gently, and steered me back to the bed with the drip in tow. I knew Miyako – a city to the south of Taro. I wondered how badly it had been affected by the tsunami. I hadn't seen any signs of damage. The nurse fussed around me, lifting my legs back into the bed and tucking the sheet tight around me.

'Thank you – you're very kind.' My voice was rusty. 'And how shall I address you?'

'I am Nurse Watanabe. The doctor will be through to see you shortly, Mr Turnbull.'

With that she gave me a short bow and was gone. I decided to do as I was told and settled back in the bed with my eyes closed, to await the doctor.

My mind was awhirl with questions – and the first of them was: where is Tashi? I shuddered with the memory of the pain he had inflicted when I arrived in Taro: the blood that had seemed to cover me; the pounding in my temples; the crown of thorns. I couldn't feel his presence. In this normal room, with sunlight striping clean sheets, the mountains seemed very far away indeed; those weeks like a dream I had awoken from, leaving nothing but a dark metallic taste on my tongue.

There was a footstep by the door and I opened my eyes to see that the promised doctor had arrived. He was thickset, in his late fifties, his shirt open at the collar, and only the stethoscope around his neck betrayed that he wasn't a fisherman or farm worker. He was accompanied by a burly man in the uniform of the local police. Seeing that I was awake he came straight to my bedside and spoke to me.

'*Ohayo Gozaimashita*! Glad to see my patient is doing so much better. Sister Watanabe tells me that you've been out of bed. How are you feeling now?'

'Good morning to you too! I'm feeling fine thank you, Doctor…?'

'Dr Murakami Masao.'

'So, since I'm ok, I guess I don't need to stay in here any more? If you could just unhook me from these machines...'

'I'm not sure that's wise, Mr Turnbull. You were brought in severely dehydrated and suffering from malnutrition – and apparently you had some kind of episode when you arrived in Taro. I wouldn't feel comfortable about discharging you until you're stronger, and we can rule out epilepsy or any other condition.'

The policeman came forward.

'Please let me introduce myself. I am Detective Ryusendo. If you're feeling well enough I'd like to ask you a few questions.'

'But I'm not under arrest?'

'You've not been formally arrested, but I would like to speak with you. You've been on the missing list since 11 March. We would like to know where you've been.'

'I thought I'd already explained this. I went running on the morning of the tsunami. I often go running up into the forest in the mornings.'

'But you didn't come back for weeks. Why now? And how did you survive up there for so long? Mr Turnbull, you've been missing for more than two months!'

I was shocked.

'Has it been that long?'

'Nine weeks to be exact. Were you staying someplace all this time? Where have you been?'

'I found a hiking lodge – a shack really – up in the mountains. It's a few hours' run from here. I used to go there sometimes. I'd left some food there.'

Ryusendo looked dubious. He leaned in towards me, his attitude like a hyena, circling his prey.

'Where is this cabin? We'll need to check it out. Have you left belongings there?'

'I could show you on a map. You'll find my pack there, a few personal things.'

'We'll send some men to check what you say. Next: why did you stay there so long? Why didn't you come back straight after the tsunami? Your wife spent a long time looking for you amongst the dead.'

'I... I can't really explain. I was unwell. I'm not sure I'm well now.'

Dr Murakami broke in.

'Detective Ryusendo! Mr Turnbull was suffering from malnutrition and hypothermia when he made contact. He's barely in any state now for these questions.'

'Ok. Then I only have one more question, Dr Murakami. Mr Turnbull – when you were found, you were shouting, "Tashi – leave me alone – why are you tormenting me?" Why did you say that, Mr Turnbull? What happened to your son, Tashi?'

My mind raced. I didn't even know myself. What could I say?

As if on cue, the sensation I had learned to associate with his presence filled me again; icy fingers seemed to caress the back of my neck. At the same time the corners of the room dimmed, as though a filter had been overlaid on my vision. I closed my eyes, willed him to leave me, but already I could hear him whispering in my ear, and feel the crown of thorns settle once again about my head, constraining it. The pain built up until I could bear it no more, and I realised that the sound of screaming was coming from me. And then a different kind of prick, real hands restraining me, pressing me back down into the welcoming sheets. Darkness comes. I welcome it.

After my arrest things seemed to happen very fast. I was taken to the nearest police station. It was the first time I had been inside a Japanese police car – or any police car in fact. I sat in the middle of the back seat, hands cuffed together, with a policeman on either side of me. Nobody spoke – least of all me. I was still processing what had happened. There was no sign of Tashi – and in fact that whole period in the mountains was rapidly taking on the aspect of a dream, or a nightmare. Meanwhile the car, the journey, the policemen and the cuffs were all too real. I knew they were taking me for further interrogation, and I wondered what I could say to them. How could I explain to them what I had been doing, when I couldn't trust my own memory? Had I really killed my child? Why? I was sure that I had made the decision to leave, to walk away. I could have stayed, been the protector.

I have to stop running away. When did I learn that? I can't remember. When did I decide that I must turn myself in? Maybe it was Tashi. Maybe Tashi is me. Listen to me talking like a crazy person; but I can't quite tell who I am any more. It was a different Harry that moved to Taro with Sachiko; a different Harry who embarked on the adventure of parenthood. It couldn't be that hard, right? I was the one who ran away. It would have been her fault then.

We have arrived. Metal doors line a long corridor. On either side I can see through the bars into identical cells. I am struck by the lack of privacy. In some cells, prisoners sit and gaze at their hands. The odd one looks up as we pass, and quickly down again. Everything is polished to a high shine. It is very quiet, and the echoes of our footsteps bounce around the unforgiving surfaces. My captors don't speak, and without warning we stop at a door that is distinguished from its fellows only by a number: 36.

Inside, a caged light bulb illuminates a stark scene. The only furniture is a rolled futon, with a folded blanket on top. In one corner there are toilet arrangements, and a tap runs into a drain in the floor. I do not know how long they plan to keep me here. There is no television, or clock, and, as I am to discover, the lights stay on 24 hours a day.

I try to settle into a rhythm, but the interrogators make it hard. Day and night it seems they are at me to confess, fill in the details in my woefully thin tale. Or tale of woe, take which you will. It won't come back. They try everything. Withholding food; withholding sleep; shouting at me day and night; playing soundtracks in my cell. Without windows, I cannot tell day from night. It's an eerie echo of what I've already been through with Tashi, and as such I feel almost immune. I've been there, done that. I'm wearing that t-shirt.

There's been no sign of Tashi since I left the hospital. I can't feel his presence at all. All this time I've hated his every manifestation, and now suddenly it feels as though there's something missing, something essential that's gone from the heart of me. He's not here. I don't think he'll ever be here again.

The other thing's gone as well. I can't cut loose in my memories and relive them like a filmstrip. All I have is disjointed snapshots and dissonant moments. And in between the interrogators come again.

'We know what you did – you told us. You've been raving and talking in your sleep. What happened after you killed the child? What did you do with the body?' It could be the delusion of a tsunami survivor without a body. They need an actual corpse it seems.

Sometimes they take me out of the cell, to a small room with a blank wall I know is a one-way mirror. Two or three men in neat uniforms conduct these sessions – usually two seated and one standing by the door, in case I make a break for it and somehow manage to circumvent the steel bars, the security doors and the vigilant duty officer by the street door. They yell things like, 'Don't lie!' and, 'You're going to hang, you know!' They kick the doors, slam the tables and walls with their fists. They are high octane. I remain calm, and this enrages them even more. Then they change tack. I am forced to spend hours of the day crouched in an uncomfortable position, cuffed with my hands behind my back; I am not allowed to use the toilet. Any sound or movement brings physical punishment. It's as though they have me in an invisible straitjacket.

I am not offered access to a lawyer. In Japan, you can be held for weeks without charge. The confession is the thing, and they like detail. A nice watertight case for the prosecutor to lay before the judge. The thing is, I wasn't playing ball. I had turned myself in, said some things that suggested that there was more to the disappearance of my child than could be explained by the tsunami alone, but that was all. I hadn't told them why, or what had happened next. They accused me of killing him, of taking his body into the wilderness. I have no memory of this; I seem to remember that he was already missing when I left. Then there were all Tashi's other stories, the films, the soundtracks, the ticker tape statistics. How could I have known about Fukushima? About the thousands lost? I couldn't know if any of it was true. How could it be true?

So I couldn't tell them any more. About where the body was, about how he had died.

After a time, in desperation, I start to talk – about Sachiko, about his birth, about our life together. About how she went away.

It came in fits and starts. Once I got started it was like somebody had turned on the tap. I couldn't stop. They kept me off guard. I would be in the middle of a sentence and they would walk out. No warning, and the one by the door would take me back to my cell. I felt my grip on reality become ever more fragile with their continuing silence. I had got up to the part where I had decided to return to Taro when they put me back in my cell for what was to be the last time, and then… and then I got transferred.

Still no lawyer. The new place seems to be a high security prison, and I am still alone in my cell. I wonder if they're keeping me in solitary on purpose, to keep me off-balance. A different set of people question me. Their uniforms, more medical than military, suggest some kind of psychiatric institution, but I've given up talking back. They don't shout at me, or leave the light on at all hours. And food arrives, regularly. I can think here.

The intercom rang, shattering the silence of the morning. It was Mrs Takamoto.

'Sachiko-chan, there's a policeman here to see you.'

Through the window Sachiko could see a police car, parked on the narrow street. She pulled on her house slippers and ran downstairs. Mrs Takamoto was standing, with the policeman next to her, waiting at the foot of the stairs. Sachiko took the last few steps slowly, legs fluttery with sudden foreboding.

She bowed to the policeman, who bowed back and introduced himself.

'Mrs Turnbull?'

It was strange to hear her married name again after all this time.

'Yes, that's me.'

'I'm sorry, but I have some news for you that might shock you, and a letter. Do you have somewhere we could talk?'

Mrs Takamoto turned away with natural delicacy and left with an excuse about laundry to be done. Sachiko was left alone with the policeman, and invited him up to her small apartment. She climbed the steps with great effort. Something heavy seemed to be weighing her down. Somehow she made it to the first floor, and her apartment door, which was still ajar. She bowed again to the policeman and invited him in.

'Sit down please, I'll just make us some tea.'

The policeman sat on the only chair. He had removed his shoes and slipped his feet into the slippers provided for guests. Sachiko sneaked glances whilst she made the tea. He was middle-aged and serious. His uniform was immaculately pressed. He'd removed his cap and gloves and placed them on the table next to the letter.

Sachiko poured the tea, and leaned against the counter top. 'Officer, do you have information about my husband?'

'Mrs Turnbull, I do. Your husband was found in Taro some days ago. He was apparently somewhat confused, as well as being dehydrated and covered with cuts and bruises. He was taken to a local hospital for treatment, and has now been moved to a detention centre.'

'Harry is still alive! And what about my son, Tashi. Does he know what became of him?'

'I'm sorry, but I don't have access to that information. Mr Turnbull appeared in Taro some days ago and was recognised by the station attendant. He had apparently been living rough in the mountains. He was emaciated and dirty. He claimed to have caught the bus from Omoto. Entries in his notebook corroborated his story. The Tohoku division got in touch with the Tokyo police and asked that we contact you personally, as it appears that Mr Turnbull absconded and hid himself for a number of weeks. Mr Turnbull had apparently asked that we not inform you of his return – but obviously, in a case like this, the courts can't respect such a wish. You have certain rights, as his spouse. It's all written down in this letter, as well as the address of the detention centre. Of course, it's up to you whether you want to see him or not.'

Sachiko was silent, gazing at the envelope until the silence became uncomfortable. The policeman took refuge in his tea and waited for her response. It took them that way sometimes and he had learned to be patient with grief.

After some time Sachiko came back to herself and found her voice. She had been looking down at her hands, fingers twisted. Now she forced herself to look the policeman in the eye. She noticed that although he was not handsome, he looked kind – the sort of person who would laugh easily.

'Thank you for your visit, Officer. Do you need an answer now?'

'No, it's fine. In fact you don't need to respond to this letter at all. Nor do you need to meet with your husband, although his medical officer may contact you and request information.'

He stood up, and replaced his hat on his head. At the door he turned and bowed to Sachiko.

'I'm sorry to be the bearer of this news, Mrs Turnbull.'

'It's your duty, I understand. Thank you again.'

Once he was gone, she took a sharp knife and slit the envelope lengthways. There was the letterhead of the Miyagi Prefectural Police. There was her name. There was the information that, after an absence of nine weeks, her husband had appeared in Taro, and had been moved to a secure facility 'for his own safety', as well as the address of the detention centre in question, and information about getting there.

It was all there – clear as day, black and white on thick headed paper – but none of it made any sense. Sachiko noticed that her hands were shaking. Made herself pour tea.

The hot liquid shocked her back into herself a little. Harry was alive! Had been alive for this whole time. What was she to think? Did he know what had happened to Tashi? Why didn't he want to see her?

There was nothing else in the envelope. The policeman had said that she could request a meeting with him, but everything in her rebelled against that idea. Why had he hidden away for all this time? Had he lost his memory? Where had he been?

Sachiko thought back to the hours spent checking morgues; pulling the sheet back on bloated, waterlogged corpses; chasing up rumours; searching and hoping for a sign that either of them had survived. Hoping at the very least for the closure of a body to mourn and lay to rest. But there had been nothing. And from that nothing she had been, and still was, building something – fragile but hopeful; a new and better life out of the freedom afforded her by a new start.

Why did this have to happen now?

There was anger – and some of the anger was inevitably at herself. If only she'd been there for them, not locked in that silent room. There was anger at Harry, and somehow less surprise than she should have felt – and why was that? And anger at Harry. And anger at Harry.

But why? There must have been a why? How could she find out the why of it all? The wherefore and how – as Harry, curse him, would have said.

Taro was a small place. A local place. Maybe she should call the local police? They might know a bit more about what had happened.

It didn't take long to find the number. Sachiko pulled out the slim file of correspondence she had kept since leaving Taro. It really hadn't been so very long ago. She found the number, but hesitated to dial.

She had to know, but she didn't know where to start. She would need to get her questions straight first. Automatically she emptied the teapot of leaves, boiled fresh water, brewed more tea.

She tried to imagine the scene. Had he really just turned up, bearded and ragged, stepped off a bus and expected everything to be as it was before? How had he been living for all that time? Why had he been arrested?

Maybe it wasn't as unlikely as it sounded. That was Harry all over. He had no idea. He'd always needed an interpreter for Japan. For ten long years she'd been just that – a buffer for his experience. Small verbal mannerisms gave him away: the way the Japanese were always 'they' whereas other long-term expats would say 'we'. So many memories flooding back. But she must stop. This wasn't doing any good. Realistically the police weren't going to release information over the phone, and she didn't really want to have to go back to Taro. The last person she wanted to see was Harry, but maybe he was the only one who could answer her questions now.

Harry was surprised, mid-morning, to be summoned from his cell. Ever since he had been transferred to the detention centre he had been kept in solitary confinement, in a tiny space barely big enough for a single futon to be rolled out. Pacing around and exercising were strictly forbidden.

Now an impassive guard opened the door and handcuffed him, before motioning him out of the cell. He followed the uniformed back of the guard down a number of corridors until he reached an area he hadn't been in before. It appeared to be an infirmary. In the hallway were several medical gurneys, and the doors off the corridor bore nameplates. The guard stopped at one of these doors and knocked. There was a muffled reply from inside, and he opened the door, before stepping aside and pushing Harry into the room before locking the door behind him.

Harry saw a couple of straight-backed chairs and another gurney. Next to it sat a healthy-looking man, with only a touch of grey in his hair and a few lines on his face to suggest he was in his fifties. He stood up as Harry entered the room and spoke in surprisingly fluent English, with just a trace of an American accent to suggest how he had come by it.

'Good morning, Mr Turnbull. My name is Dr Kitahara. I've been assigned to evaluate your mental condition. Please lie down on that bed over there.'

Harry did as he was asked and looked over at Dr Kitahara expectantly. He was learning not to speak out of turn. It could often earn you a clip around the head, and the guards tended to be heavy-handed. The doctor, however, seemed cut from a different cloth – and any change was welcome after days of monotony crouched in an uncomfortable position in his small cell.

'How are you feeling today, Mr Turnbull?'

Harry answered carefully.

'I'm feeling fine, Doctor. At least as well as can be expected. It's nice to meet you – however I have to tell you I'm not sure I've much more to say about what's happened to me than I've already said. There's a lot I don't remember.'

'Actually that's exactly where I come in. I'm very good at helping people to remember things that they've forgotten. Memory can be the best healer there is.'

Harry's face darkened, and a touch of the old rage showed in his eyes.

'I don't know about that. Some things are probably best forgotten.'

Dr Kitahara was abruptly formal.

'I will be the judge of that. Meanwhile, I have been asked to come down and assess you. Your notes mention that you've been experiencing some hallucinations. Can you describe them to me?'

Harry didn't answer. His expression was watchful and guarded. As the silence lengthened, Dr Kitahara tried another tack.

'Mr Turnbull, you were arrested in Taro after having been missing, presumed dead, for nine weeks. You claimed to have been living in a cabin in the woods, in between bouts of wandering – and investigators have subsequently found traces of your presence that confirm this. You also claim that you decided to walk out on your family for no reason, conveniently just before a tsunami destroyed your home. You have been heard arguing with yourself and with a being you believe is the ghost of your child – even though you claim he was already missing when you decided to run away. Mr Turnbull, we are here to discover the truth behind these stories. Perhaps not today, but we will get there in the end. You'll do better to cooperate with me. The consequences for you will be severe if you don't.'

Harry looked beaten, and his voice was soft and hesitant when he replied.

'It's true. I do seem to remember contradictory things. There were times I blacked out. Big gaps – like a darkness. I was seeing things that weren't there – at least, they shouldn't have been possible.'

'Your son...' Dr Kitahara prompted.

'Like Tashi, but not really him. An older version. Tashi was only three months old when he... This Tashi was able to speak to me. And he wasn't very nice either. I've been seeing him pretty much since I left Taro. He's not here now.'

'How do you know he's not here now?'

'I can't feel him. It gets cold when he's around, like chilly fingers down the back of my neck. Can we talk about something else?'

Harry was getting visibly agitated. Dr Kitahara decided to try a different strategy.

'Mr Turnbull, have you ever heard of regression therapy?'

'Isn't it some kind of hypnosis technique, where you get people to relive past experiences?'

'That's exactly correct. I need you to sign this form, which states that you agree to take part in therapy. This is for your own benefit. You have been charged with the murder of your child.'

He passed a form clipped to a board over to Harry. The form was in Japanese, with just a space and a cross to indicate where Harry was to sign.

Harry hesitated, trying to puzzle out the kanji.

Dr Kitahara spoke again, his tone more reasonable this time.

'Mr Turnbull, this is for your own good. Murder carries a death sentence. Or we may discover that you are innocent. Survivor's guilt is a well-documented phenomenon. Who's to say that you didn't imagine the whole thing, after the trauma of, as you thought, losing your whole family to the tsunami?'

He looked questioningly at Harry, who sighed and picked up the pen.

'Ok, Dr Kitahara – I'm going to take you at your word. And it's not like I have a choice anyway. I'll sign.'

Harry was with Dr Kitahara in a small room, him on a recliner, Dr Kitahara on an upright chair. Dr Kitahara noted that Harry seemed very restless. His fingers drummed on the arms of the chair, and he blinked often. Occasionally he seemed to shy at something invisible. He was anything but relaxed – it was as though he was on guard, in fear of an enemy.

'Take a deep breath. Hold that breath… and exhale. And as you breathe, feel the relaxation flooding your body.' Gradually Dr Kitahara's steady voice took him under.

Harry became a little calmer. He no longer looked as though he was about to take flight. He relaxed into the cushions and stopped drumming his fingers on the arm of the chair.

'That's it. Nice deep breaths. And as you breathe, you can feel yourself becoming more relaxed, here in this safe place, with my voice to guide you. And when I speak to you, you will be able to answer me.'

Dr Kitahara continued in a low monotone.

'Keep breathing deeply. With every breath you inhale and exhale you go deeper and deeper, still with my voice to guide you.'

Calm and measured, his words like a metronome, talking Harry down.

'Hold. And release. Hold and release, and every breath that you release makes you go deeper and deeper, until all you can hear is my voice guiding you. Deeper and deeper.'

'Every sound that you hear outside this room just reassures you that everything is fine, and you go deeper, and deeper, you are more relaxed, more peaceful. All you can hear now is my voice, as we go deep on this journey together.'

'As we speak, I'm going to ask you to rewind your mind to the day of the tsunami, it was a Friday, 11 March. And I want you to go back to that moment, and when you feel that you've arrived there, I want you to signal to me that you're at that place, on Friday, 11 March, by lifting your index finger, and saying, "I'm here". And your finger will stay lifted until I say, "Thank you" and acknowledge it. Can you do that for me now?'

Dr Kitahara repeated the same words again, starting from, 'I'm going to ask you to rewind your mind' until he got to the final words, 'Can you do that for me now?' He waited a few seconds to see if Harry made any response to his words. He seemed to be sleeping,

'Once again, going deeper and deeper, back and back, week by week, until we get to that Friday, on 11 March, in Taro. And as we arrive there, your index finger will rise up, and will stay up until I say, "Thank you, Harry" and you'll say, "I'm here".'

This time, almost before he had finished the sentence, Harry's finger was twitching.

'I'm here.'

'Thank you, Harry. You can put your finger down now. Harry, can you tell me where you are?'

'I'm in our living room.'

'Thank you, Harry. And is anyone else there with you?'

'The baby's here. He's watching me. And she's here too, Sachiko, in the next room. I don't know if she's awake.'

'What happens next, Harry?'

'I can't stand him watching me. It doesn't feel right, like he's inserted himself into the situation. Like someone spliced extra scenes into a film reel. I close my eyes. I can't stand his gaze. It's like he knows too much.'

'What does he know, Harry?'

'I know it's bad. It's something to do with her. Something she's done.'

Dr Kitahara wasn't sure what to make of this, and Harry was quiet, at rest, waiting for another question. During the whole session his expression hadn't changed, although his voice betrayed the strain of memory – it was cracked with emotion. Dr Kitahara templed his fingers under his chin, wondering what to try next, when suddenly Harry started speaking again.

'The room is shaking. It's a quake – a bad one. I need to get out. I've got the stuff all ready. I've got a place to go. I grab the stuff and start walking – just walk out the door and keep going. Then I start running. Everything's falling apart around me. I can't keep on my feet, but I just keep going straight out of town, until I've left it all behind. There's rocks falling in the mountains, but at least that awful grinding noise has stopped. I don't stop running until I get to my hiding place.'

'It's peaceful up there, and I'm feeling good. I start getting things ready for the night – collecting wood for the fire, and then I trip and then he's there – laughing at me, and at first I don't believe what I'm seeing, but he won't go away.'

Harry stopped talking and shuddered into stillness. The doctor wasn't sure how much more to push him, but decided to make one last push, to try to get more information. He leaned in closer to Harry, and spoke quietly.

'What happened next, Harry – what do you remember?'

There was no answer and Harry just lay there with his eyes closed. Dr Kitahara tried again.

'Harry, if you can hear me, and you're still in that moment, lift your left index finger now.'

Moments passed, and there was no response. In the dim room the very air was still, silent but for their regular breathing and the tick of a clock on the wall. Dr Kitahara watched Harry, who gave every indication of being deep in trance. He considered what to do next. He could try to force the issue, by taking Harry deeper, but that approach could also backfire; you can't force someone to act against their deepest will, even with hypnosis – and trying to bludgeon himself against Harry's will could end up with him building mental defences. These would have to be painstakingly broken down before they could move ahead with the therapy. Dr Kitahara decided to stop for the day. He started talking again in a low voice.

'Harry, we're going to bring you back to wakefulness now. I'm going to start counting backwards slowly, and as I count you'll be visualising climbing a set of stairs, towards the light. Can you do that for me, Harry? Visualise climbing those stairs towards that light. And when you reach the top you will wake, and you'll feel as calm and rested as though you'd just had a good night's sleep. I'll start counting now.

'Twenty...

'Nineteen...

'Eighteen... seventeen... sixteen... fifteen... fourteen...

'You're halfway up the stairs now... you can see the light at the top, and when you reach the top you'll come back once again into wakefulness, and feel as rested as though you had slept for eight hours.

'Thirteen... twelve... eleven... ten... nine... eight... seven... six... five...

'Only a few more steps to go now, and you're feeling lighter and lighter, energised as though the weights have been removed from your feet.'

Harry was starting to stir now, and his breathing was coming quicker. His fingers twitched on the armrests of the chair, and his feet shifted. Dr Kitahara continued his measured count.

'Four... nearly there now. Three. Last couple of steps... two. One. And we're back in the room.'

Harry's eyes fluttered and slowly opened. He stared in front of him, and his hands gripped the seat rests so hard his knuckles turned white, and Dr Kitahara wondered what demons he was negotiating with in his head. Then he seemed to come back to himself, shuddering slightly and turning his head to face Dr Kitahara. His face was calm again, and his voice even.

'So, Dr Kitahara – was that a useful session? What was I able to remember? Should I be able to recall it now?'

'I think the session went well – you're a good subject for hypnosis it seems. We'll prepare the tape and I'll be able to report back to you when we've had a chance to review the session. Thanks for your time, Mr Turnbull.'

'Isn't it strange I can't remember it now? Oh well, maybe it will come back. I'll look forward to whatever you can tell me, Dr Kitahara.'

'It won't be long – I promise. Meanwhile, we'd better get you back to your cell, unless there was anything else you wanted to talk about right now?'

'I think I'm good for now, Dr Kitahara. See you soon.'

As he got up to go, Dr Kitahara was freshly aware of the bulk of him – he was a tall man, and not heavy, but solidly built. He didn't hold himself in a menacing way, but Kitahara sensed a capacity for violence in him – a strength barely contained. He crossed to the door, unlocked it, and signalled to the guard across the hall, who got up, ready to escort Harry back to his room. They shook hands formally, and Harry meekly followed the guard down the hall. From behind, in his loose pyjamas and slippers, in which even the most determined walker had a tendency to shuffle, he appeared to have a certain fragility, belying the earlier impression of his strength. Dr Kitahara was too shaken by what he had heard to include it in his mental picture of Harry Turnbull.

He would have no choice but to pass the tapes to the prison authorities, even though he couldn't tell at this point whether what Harry seemed to remember was actually true. It was all on tape, and they would be fully within their rights to demand the tape as evidence. A story told whilst under hypnosis isn't legally binding, and there was no proof, except for Harry's story – possibly the fantasy of a madman. It was possible that his mental instability would save him – under Article 39 of the criminal code, penalties could be reduced for a 'weak-minded person' and, in the absence of Tashi's body, nothing could be proven.

In his waking moments, between those strange episodes when he argued with a person that no one else could see, he seemed sane, intelligent, polite. Now a darker side was emerging.

三五

It was late afternoon when Hiromichi called. Sachiko was startled, because previously they had communicated in person, or by text. It was the first time he had called her. She didn't answer the phone, just stared at the screen stupidly, wondering what the call might portend. Then she thought to press the answer button, and there was Hiromichi's voice. He sounded upset.

'Sachiko, I'm not sure if you've seen the news today?'

No 'hello'. Straight to the point – and unusually direct for Hiromichi.

'No – I haven't got around to getting a television set yet. What did you see?'

'Your husband was... is... called Harry Turnbull isn't he? It seems he has turned up in Taro, very much alive. Did you know about this? Were you going to tell me about it?'

His voice rang in her ear and Sachiko pulled the handset away slightly. She didn't know what to reply. Yes, she had known. For all of 48 hours! And who would have thought the case would have attracted media interest so fast. It must be because he was a foreigner – and the newsmen, and their public, were bored of stories about power plants. All he had done was run away.

'Sachiko? Are you still there?'

'I'm here. I'm sorry – I only found out a couple of days ago. It was such a shock. I still don't know what to think.'

The doorbell rang.

'Listen – I've got to go – the doorbell – I'm sorry. I'll call you when they've gone. Bye.'

Sachiko hung up and went to the window. Below, she could just make out two men, casually dressed, one carrying a video camera and a big fluffy boom microphone. She assumed they were press. She didn't want to talk to them. She would have to phone Hiro-chan back. But he had sounded so angry. What right had he to be angry? She was angry. With herself, for allowing it all to happen; with Harry for running away, for destroying their family, for, she had to admit, systematically bullying and grinding her down through the years of their marriage. It had been assumed she would give up work when they married – even though that was no longer expected. Harry had loved coming home to an immaculate house and dinner on the table. At first she had not even minded giving up her career – it wasn't as though her work was that exciting, and in the first flush of love after their wedding she had enjoyed playing house, preparing the tastiest dinners for him, watching as he wrote and reading what he had produced. That had changed as he had grown more secretive, and started refusing to show her his work.

No, Hiro-chan should not be angry. They had barely scratched the surface of each other. She was just learning to be herself again.

Sachiko peered out of the window. Mrs Takamoto wasn't home and she didn't think the pressmen would doorstep any of the other residents. With no one to speak to perhaps they wouldn't linger. Sachiko had never liked talking on the telephone – away from the nuance of gesture and sound, reliant on the inadequate mechanical reproduction of human intention. She intended to go and see Hiromichi in person, and find out what was making him so angry.

The next morning Sachiko rose early, as usual, and went to work. She wasn't sure if it was the appropriate thing to do, whether she should call Hiromichi; but she didn't want to speak to him on the phone. She needed to be able to gauge his eyes. She hoped the normality of work would soothe her. And, in fact, the menial tasks induced in her a kind of meditative state, so that she was able to feel calmer than she had at any time since she had discovered that Harry was still living.

As soon as she finished she hurried straight to the bookshop – not even bothering to go home and change first. When she arrived Hiromichi was serving an elderly man, and she waited in a side alcove until he was done, idly browsing through the stock on show there. As soon as the bell tinkled behind the departing customer she came out of the alcove, and went up to the counter. Hiromichi said nothing, just motioned her through the curtain behind the counter to his private quarters. Sachiko sat awkwardly on the single chair until he came through to take up a place facing her, his back to the kitchen counter.

Sachiko looked down at her hands, at the fingers twisted together, waiting for him to say something, whilst at the same time knowing he would not. She was the one who had come to see him; the onus was on her to start the conversation. She had thought long and hard about what she should say. It had seemed so clear that morning, whilst she was polishing floors and cleaning bathrooms. Now, with Hiromichi in front of her, it felt as though she had been struck dumb. But she had to start somewhere.

She looked up and met his gaze. The kind twinkle was missing from his eyes. He looked hurt, and defensive, and angry, and he was holding himself stiffly. She hadn't seen him this way before.

'I had to come and see you. It didn't feel right to leave it that way, or to talk about all of... this... on the phone.'

She waited for a response, but he only nodded. It seemed like it was up to her to make the next move too.

'Hiromichi-san...' the honorific felt strange, after their intimacy.

'... I wanted to apologise for the way that things have turned out. The way that you found out about Harry. I promise you that I never dreamed that he might still be alive. It came as quite a shock to me too. I thought I was alone in the world. I have been trying to make a new life for myself – and now this. What we have really means a lot to me. I feel like it means a lot to you too.'

He looked away, fixed his eyes on a point on the wall behind her. There was nothing there but faded paper. Eventually he spoke, still refusing to meet her eyes.

'Will you go to see him?'

Now it was Sachiko's turn to look away – down at the fingers that twisted and intertwined as if to demonstrate the tangled knot that had replaced her heart.

'I don't know. I've been trying to decide. I wanted to ask you how you felt about it.'

His answer was quick and bitter.

'Why would you want to ask me? We're not married.'

Sachiko was nonplussed. What could Hiromichi mean? Did what

they had together mean nothing to him? She wanted to ask, but it didn't feel right to be so direct. She hunted around for the words to explain.

'It's been very hard, settling into this new life, making a routine for myself. I would not have been able to do that without you, and Mrs Takamoto. You've been so kind. Between you, you've kept me sane and helped me to move on. That's why I wanted to come and see you today. I wanted to talk about where we go from here.'

'It's the moving on that worries me, actually. What about your child? Did you find out what happened with Tashi? And how can you just ignore your husband now that he's turned up? That's the part I'm struggling to understand. How can I trust you if you just move on every time a situation becomes difficult? I didn't grow up that way – I could never leave my parents, turn my back on everything that made me what I am. I'm sorry, Sachiko – but I can't feel comfortable with that – with you – knowing that you've been able to forget two families already. How can I trust you, knowing you'll just walk away from me too?'

Sachiko kept her eyes downcast during this speech. He spoke in a low voice – passionately, but without anger. She could tell he too had been considering what to say. Had he let her have the first word out of consideration? A last chance at reprieve before he finished their affair?

'But I didn't abandon my family. They were stolen from me by the tsunami.'

'So you say, and I'm sorry to seem harsh, but I think there's more to it than that. There must be – or you'd have run straight back to Harry when you got that letter from the police. What else is there, Sachiko? What is it that made you cut yourself off from your parents, and now Harry too? You appeared so fragile when we first met – but it seems you're stronger than you look. You frighten me, Sachiko.'

'Don't be afraid, Hiro-chan. It's true, I've cut myself off from my parents. It felt like the right thing to do at the time – and I know that seems strange to someone like you. But I felt like I needed to escape from everything they expected from me. I was being pressured into a way of life I wasn't ready to accept, moulded into a stranger. Didn't you ever feel that way? You inherited this bookshop from your father – didn't you ever want to leave? Do something else?'

'No. It's not just about duty for me. I love this place. All I've ever wanted is to be here. I've no plans except to continue a way of life that's all I have ever known. Have you never been happy, Sachiko?'

'I was happy, Hiro-chan, with you – at least I was learning to be happy. But now I don't know if the kind of happiness that you have to offer is what I really need. It's all so civilised: chatting about books; drinking fine coffee; listening to the latest from the Kronos Quartet. Don't you ever feel like they're mental crutches? Like you're experiencing life at one remove? I thought we had found something meaningful – something true. But maybe I'm wrong. Maybe we're just living out a cliché. That's not what I mean. Oh – I hate this!'

Hiromichi heard her out, but his white knuckled grip on the counter behind him betrayed his true feelings. She could tell he was angry – she had gone too far, and anyway it wasn't what she meant to say. She groped for the words and then continued.

'I felt like I was getting better – that life was getting better. Can't you see – I'm not turning my back on anything by being with you. I realised that for all those years I was married to an emotional terrorist. Being with you has taught me to be comfortable with both sides of myself. The one that's intrigued by the treasures of the West, and the one that will always be Japanese. If nothing else I owe that to you.'

'That's exactly what bothers me. It's like you've become a tourist – like you're looking in from the outside at all the quaint little people. But you don't really care – it can't affect you. The first time I saw you I thought you were dancing in a bubble. I was right, but not in the way I thought. You are untouchable. I can't break through to where you are, the heart of you.'

Sachiko looked at him, mutely. She felt as though she'd been here before – like a doll, like an imperceptible woman, created anew by whoever beheld her. She could feel herself receding – the distance that beckoned her back to that place: the little room. The whole situation took on a kind of unreality – as though this were another in the long chain of people who had wanted to shape her in the image that they had conceived of her. And was she ready for this latest incarnation? It was safe, it was lovely. She could do what was expected of her. She could go and see Harry, and report back, and make up with her parents and probably patch up the rift that had appeared in their relationship. She could be the paper woman. But there would be nothing inside.

The bell tinkled, signalling the arrival of a customer. Hiromichi looked quickly to the side, towards the curtain that hid the shop. It was a signal, and Sachiko gathered herself together whilst he went through to the front. She heard the low mumble of voices, and then they receded, as Hiromichi presumably left the counter to go and find something the customer had requested. She wondered if she should wait. But what would be the point? It felt as though something had broken in their relationship, like a cracked vase that gives a false note when tapped.

Now was not the time for this conversation – neither of them wanted such a public display of their pain; it was too private. Sachiko got up and pulled back the curtain. There was Hiromichi, deep in conversation with a young man about some new *manga* that had come in. He seemed calm, and much as she had seen him when she had still been merely a customer. Quietly she walked around the counter and went out. The bell tinkled once again. The customer barely looked up, but Hiromichi watched her slim back receding through the door before turning back to serve him.

三六

Dr Kitahara continued his sessions with Harry over the following weeks. During this time he developed a growing conviction that something was wrong with his story. Something that Harry could not admit even to himself.

They went through Harry's notebook together, and talked about the entries that he had made. Dr Kitahara began to think that there was more than one Harry, and was never sure which he would encounter at their sessions. There was the polite Englishman, who tried to explain why he had chosen to leave when he did and why he had been preparing a refuge in the forest. There was another, less lucid Harry, whose eyes shifted when questioned; who held himself differently; who didn't seem to know who he was, or what he remembered. The notebook referred to conversations with Tashi, and Harry's belief that his son had come back as a ghost. At first Dr Kitahara assumed that these were just the delusions of a mind under pressure but, as time went on, and as other people across Tohoku began to report cases of haunting and possession, he became less sure of his diagnosis.

There was simply no explanation for other entries in Harry's diary. How, for example, had Harry known about the power station at Fukushima, the abandoned towns and the destruction of hundreds of miles of coastline, if he had been hiding in the mountains with no contact with the outside world?

The sessions continued without a breakthrough until one day Harry rolled off the couch where he had been lying and dropped to all fours on the floor. He began writhing and twisting, his face set in a snarl. Suddenly he arched his back and put both hands behind his head as if he were trying to claw away someone that was holding onto his neck.

'Get off, get off, you're dead. They're all dead. Everyone's dead. Everything's gone. Why don't you stay dead? Why don't you leave me alone?'

Dr Kitahara bent down and felt for Harry's wrist. His pulse was racing, and his eyes, when he turned his head, seemed to look right through him. He bucked again and rolled onto his back, holding his hands up as if to ward off an attacker. His breath came in short gasps.

'I can't... breathe... hands... at... my... throat... strangling me.'

Dr Kitahara tried to restrain him, gently calling his name quietly, and then with more force.

'Harry. Can you hear me? Mr Turnbull.'

It was as if he wasn't there. Harry started to writhe and buck more violently still, and lash out with his fists.

'No, Tashi – no – leave me alone. You're not meant to be here. You're not allowed to be here. You're gone.'

'Mr Turnbull!'

Louder this time. Dr Kitahara grabbed Harry by the shoulder, and squeezed. The muscles were hard and tendons stood out on his neck, as if he were straining under a great weight. He groaned and started clawing at the floor, for all the world as if he were trying to escape through it.

Dr Kitahara was torn whether to call the prison guards to restrain him. They would almost certainly punish Harry for making a disturbance, but he was concerned that he might hurt himself if he was left like this for much longer. Then, just as suddenly as it had come on, the fit passed away. Harry gave one last shout and collapsed on the floor.

Immediately Dr Kitahara was by his side. Harry's pulse was already slowing, and he appeared to be asleep, his features relaxed from the rictus of moments before. Dr Kitahara waited a few moments, but there was no sign of him waking naturally. Around him was the silence of the infirmary wing, and, although he knew there was a guard outside the door, there had been no knock of enquiry. It seemed as though the disturbance had passed unnoticed. Dr Kitahara retired to his chair, and sat, watching his patient and deep in thought. Now the really dark secrets were coming out – the things that Harry could not admit to himself, except through the medium of hallucination. And yet... Dr Kitahara had heard the rumours. Taxi drivers picking up ghostly passengers; spirits stalking the deserted streets of

Ishinomaki, Miyako and other towns that had been worst hit by the tsunami.

He was not a superstitious man, but he began to wonder if what he had just encountered was a ghost. Could it be? Even if in the unlikely event this was true, and not just the product of a disordered mind unable to come to terms with guilt, it would have little impact on the legal process. Harry would be sentenced just the same.

三七

Sachiko received a call from Hiroko.

'Sachiko-chan – I saw the news – I had to call you. Is everything ok?'

It wasn't a brilliant line; static crackled so that Sachiko could barely hear her.

'Hiroko – it's good to hear your voice. Things have been better. But how are you?'

'Well, you know. As well as we can be. We're still living in Kuji; my son's at a new school and Mama-chan is looking after him whilst I go to work. I got a job in a supermarket. It pays the bills. But I wanted to check on you. I saw on the news that your husband has been found?'

'Well... not exactly "found" – he turned himself in.'

'I can't believe he's been alive all this time! Have you spoken to him yet?'

'No... he's being held in a detention centre whilst they investigate his case.'

'But what for? They said on the news that he's been charged...'

Hiroko sounded confused. She paused for a moment, and Sachiko could feel that she was searching for the right words.

'Sachiko, I'm so sorry to pry... I just thought you seemed so alone and that you might need a friend.'

'Don't be sorry, Hiroko. I'm not quite sure what to think myself. I've just about managed to get used to being on my own, and now suddenly everything has changed again. Hiroko, they told me Tashi didn't die in the tsunami. That's why they've arrested him. He's being charged with murder.'

At the other end of the line Hiroko was silent. Japan is a country with very little crime, and a conviction rate of over 90%. If Harry had been charged, that meant he would almost certainly be found guilty.

'Have you told your parents?'

'No... I've been thinking about getting in touch, and then this happened. I'm not sure how they would feel about me contacting them now. The shame of course…'

'Sachiko, they are your own blood. And I'm sure they'd understand that it's not your fault.'

Sachiko thought about what she'd said, and tried to picture her stern and traditional father's reaction to the news.

'I think they'd say, "You married him. You have only yourself to blame, but we have to pay for your actions."'

'Hmm.' Hiroko didn't sound convinced. 'I suppose you know your parents best. So what will you do? Will you go and see him?'

Sachiko tried to picture how that would be. Failed. She had never been to a prison.

'I don't know, maybe I should. I need to think about it. Anyway, I don't really know how these things work. Whether you're allowed to visit.'

'The wife always is. Sachiko, you need to know why it happened, why he left you, what happened with Tashi – or you'll always be left asking questions.'

Sachiko moaned.

'Oh I'm sure you're right, Hiroko. It's just all so sudden. And it's good to have a friend to talk to about it. Mrs Takamoto, the caretaker here, is very nice, but you know how it is when someone's in trouble with the law. I don't really know what to say to her.'

'I'm sure she'll understand. It's not like you've done anything wrong, is it? I mean, you're the victim in this situation. And your parents too. Sachiko, I hope you don't mind me saying this, because we haven't known each other for very long, but it feels like you're trying to hide yourself away; like you have an instinct to run when things get difficult. It's hard, but I'm learning the trick is to fight the battle. It's the only way we can go on.'

'I know you're right, Hiroko. You've made me feel much better. I'll try to think about what you said.'

'You do that. And remember – you're the innocent one. Let me know what you plan to do next, ok?'

'I will, Hiroko. And thanks again.'

'That's ok. I'd better go, or I'll run out of credit. I'll call you again soon. Bye!'

Hiroko rang off, and Sachiko sat, with the phone in her hand, thinking about what she had said. Hiroko was right. She would have to go and see him.

三八

Time passed and winter came again. The wheels of justice turned slowly. Sachiko had received permission to visit Harry in prison. She made the long journey from Tokyo, watching as the city was replaced by the remembered colours of Tohoku; the brown rice fields, scattered with dirty snow; dark shuttered villages, nestled between shadowy forests that had lost their autumn colour; and wide, slow rivers. Too quickly it seemed she reached her destination.

The gate was forbidding, and the avenue leading up to the prison was stark, with swathes of leaves turning to mush on the damp ground.

She gave her name, showed her ID, and then sat down to wait for her turn. It was a longish wait. She had over half an hour to reflect, there in that antiseptic waiting room, on what had brought her here. It had only been months since they had seen each other, but for Sachiko it felt like several lifetimes had passed. There had been the tsunami, and that awful moment where the dark water engulfed her; and the even worse time after she had awoken – the dawning realisation that she would never see her child and husband again, that there would never be closure of those issues. It had been made bearable, in a way, amidst the loss of thousands – a kind of solidarity in grief. And she had moved past it, as they had, into a new life.

The guard called her name, and she found herself unconsciously holding her breath as she gathered herself up to follow him through the door marked 'visiting rooms – entrance'. She tried to summon up an image of Harry, to imagine what he looked like now – but even creating a picture of his face was a struggle. She watched the back of the guard in front of her. He opened a door, and all of a sudden Harry was there.

She had stopped noticing what he looked like when Tashi was born. There had been the post-natal amnesia, then the depression, and her gradual withdrawal. She realised it must have been over a year since she'd actually, really looked at him. She studied his face, and the changes there. He looked thin, and his skin had darkened, as if weathered by cold. New lines creased his brow and forehead. His nose seemed beakier, and his eyes more deep-set. His hair was still thick, but greying at the sides. And what would Harry see? He was studying her at least as intently.

Sachiko found herself examining her heart to see if she still felt something for him, but there was nothing there. Odd – how could she ever have had feelings for this man? With a shock she realised that now she found him physically ugly. Where once his height had been attractive, now he just seemed gangling, like a giant spider folded in its web. She compared Harry's lanky frame to Hiromichi's compact person. Distantly she noticed that Harry's fingernails had been chewed down to grubby stumps, the knuckles raw and raised. She hadn't realised that she was so fastidious. She found a vague memory of having been entranced by his wild curls and his long fingers. It was gone now.

Part of the reason that the visit was so stilted was the requirement of the prison authorities that all their conversation be in Japanese. Harry had picked up a working knowledge of the language, but he and Sachiko had always communicated in English. The presence of the prison guard listening to every word was both comforting and constraining. Comforting, because she didn't know quite how she felt about being in the same space as Harry, knowing what she did now. Despite the underlying animosity between them there had rarely been any overt violence in their relationship; it had manifested in silences, or in careful statements. But according to the police this man had murdered their child, and then calmly jogged out of town, leaving her to be swept up in the aftermath of the tsunami. She had been angry with him for deserting her, for the worry and anguish she had experienced, but now she felt numb, as if half of her brain were frozen. She didn't know what to think. How to react. It didn't feel right. There was something nagging at her subconscious, like the feeling you get when you know you've left the house without something important, but you can't identify what. They carefully skirted around the topic of what Harry had done, and his answers, oddly stilted in his bad Japanese, gave Sachiko few clues as to what had motivated him. He didn't seem to feel remorse, or sadness for what they had lost. He appeared curiously divorced from the conversation; his eyes constantly drifting over her left shoulder, as if taking cues from an invisible person behind her.

They talked about the present.

'So, are you comfortable here? Are they treating you ok? What about the food?'

'The food's ok – rice, pickles, vegetables – the usual. If you work, you get more – especially for manual work. And I don't mind working. Actually – it makes the time go quicker. The cell is comfortable enough. It's not too bad so long as I behave myself. It's less pleasant if you cross the line.'

Sachiko tried to imagine what he meant by that, but didn't like to ask further. She changed the subject.

'So, do you know what will happen next?'

'Well, they've set a date for the actual trial. My lawyer's gathering evidence. It's likely to be in a month or so, and meanwhile I have to stay right here. There's a small matter of a missing body. They're looking for it now apparently.'

Sachiko watched him, paralysed, like a rabbit in the headlights. She didn't know quite how to react. She hadn't thought it would be this bad.

'They need a body you know. Otherwise I could just have cracked and imagined the whole thing; the trauma of the tsunami; Tashi following me around the mountains like some hungry ghost, like a *gaki* out of the old stories. My lawyer wants to try that angle. Apparently I can still withdraw my confession before it actually goes to trial. I'm not sure if I want to hang. It was only one murder, but I killed a child – and apparently I haven't shown nearly enough remorse.'

Sachiko gasped, and Harry cracked the first smile she'd seen since she arrived. It didn't reach his eyes.

Sachiko looked up at the clock on the wall. She couldn't believe that only 10 minutes had passed since she'd arrived. It felt like longer. She gazed across the table at Harry. The silence stretched out, and the guard reminded them of his presence by shifting from foot to foot. She wondered what he made of this, whether he had an opinion either way, or was so hardened to criminals and their evil deeds that he didn't care.

Harry hadn't asked what Sachiko had been doing over the last seven months – where she had been living, or how she had survived. He must know that she had moved to Tokyo, but he seemed to have no curiosity as to what she was doing there. Sachiko didn't volunteer any information. She was not sure where things stood with Hiromichi, and it felt too private. They both sat, silently, looking anywhere but at each other for a long five minutes, and then time was up. Harry stood up and let himself be led to the door; he waited patiently whilst the guard opened it, and ushered him through. He didn't look back, and Sachiko waited until he was out of sight before she stood up and went through the door marked 'visitor – exit', with a sign of a running man.

三九

Sachiko hadn't heard from Hiromichi since their last, heated, conversation when she received a message from him. It was characteristically brief:

'Would you like to come to the Sankeien Garden with me tomorrow? It's a beautiful place, even at this time of year when there's no blossom. Let me know, and I'll pick you up at 10am.'

The next day dawned bright and clear. Sachiko rose early and dressed with care. She had already been out to get supplies, and took the time to make a couple of *bento* boxes for herself and Hiromichi. It had been a long time since she had assembled a lunch in this way; normally she didn't bother when she went to work – she'd make do with *onigiri* bought from the convenience store on the way to work. Harry had been the last person she had made lunch for. Sachiko chose her dishes carefully – *tamagoyaki*, because it was so easy to make and the sweet omelette was comforting to eat; *onigiri*, seasoned rice balls that were the perfect hand-food. She took her time, arranging the rice, pickles, cutlets and *tamagoyaki* just so, and tried not to fret at the plastic lunchboxes, bought hastily in a hundred-yen shop around the corner, and the lack of a *furoshiki* to wrap them in. Still, Hiromichi would understand that she hadn't had a chance to replace such things. She thought of his sparse bachelor's apartment. He didn't seem the type to care about belongings too much. They had that much in common – of all the things lost in the tsunami, there were hardly any she missed. She remembered her favourite lunchbox. It had been a rare gift from her mother – a handcrafted bamboo *bento* that she had used since starting high school.

At 10am precisely the intercom went, and looking down she could see Hiromichi waiting below – his dark head, the patient stance of him. She paused a moment, there at the window. It was a moment of choice. Not that she wouldn't go with him now, to the garden, but it felt as though something had been irrevocably damaged, the last time they met, in Hiromichi's shop. Sachiko wanted to be sure that she was acting under her own volition: not because it was what was expected of her, or because she was trying to smooth things over, to capitulate. She'd been doing that for too long. Now was the time to be herself; to discover herself. And if she liked the future that they could build together, then that's the one she would choose.

Maybe she was reading too much into his invitation. The choice of location seemed significant. Sachiko had heard of Sankeien Garden. Hidden away in an obscure suburb, it had been gifted by the Hara family to the city of Yokohama, and was famed for a collection of historic buildings, that had been painstakingly reconstructed around the margins of a lake. It was the kind of place where couples went; a perfect place to picnic.

Turning away from the window she gathered the neat packages into a bag. She took her coat from the hook by the door and made her way down to street level.

四十

Sachiko hadn't been sure what he would be like, after their previous angry parting, but Hiromichi smiled when he saw her, and, reaching out, took the bag with their lunches in it from her. They took the train to Yokohama, and a bus from there to Sankeien Garden.

At this time of year the gardens were quiet – the calm vista of the lake was surrounded by cherry trees not now in blossom, with the peaks of the pagoda and the curved roofs of traditional farmhouses peeking out from behind tall stands of bamboo. They went through the gate, and took a path that led upwards, to where there was a vantage point over the gardens, and where it was quiet, and private.

A young couple, graceful in traditional dress, posed for wedding photographs on a bridge over one of the many ponds. Their posture was rigidly formal, but even from a distance Sachiko could see the love that bound them, and momentarily wished that she had been that kind of bride. Her wedding to Harry had been legal as soon as they had filed for marriage at their local government office, and the simple dinner party that followed was their only celebration. This couple looked as though they were planning on going for the full Shinto ceremony; the bride painted white from head to toe, symbolising her virginity, and wearing the traditional white hood that all but concealed her face; the groom straight-backed and slim in formal kimono. When Sachiko had married Harry they had dressed down – neither had been much into the idea of marriage as an institution, but it would keep immigration off Harry's back. And they had loved each other then, or so it seemed. But what had that love been? She compared it to the feeling she had when she was with Hiromichi, casting sidelong glances at him as they strolled along.

Hiromichi had dressed simply, in a black jumper and dark jeans. Neat shoes. His hair was a little long, and fell over his eyes when he was looking down, as now, picking his way along the winding paths. Her eyes had been at Harry's chest level but Hiromichi was only a little taller than her, and she could meet his gaze without raising her head. She looked down quickly as she nearly stumbled over one of the twisted roots that meandered over the dirt path they were following and felt a gentle hand at her elbow, steadying her.

As they wandered around the buildings that had been transported from all over Japan and reconstructed there, Sachiko and Hiromichi were silent. Neither wanted to be the first to speak, to shatter what suddenly felt so fragile between them.

Taking a fork in the path, they headed up a narrow lane lined with trees until they came to an old house, filled with period furniture and implements of farming. At the entrance they both removed their shoes, and left them in cubbyholes that had been worn by generations of use, before climbing over the threshold and entering the farmhouse itself. They had the building more or less to themselves. It was designed in the old style, with earthen floors, and was very gloomy inside. The only light came from papered windows that left the corners in shadow. It was the kind of house a farmer might have lived in a hundred years before.

Next to each object were small neatly typed labels, hard to read in the dim light. They leaned in dutifully to read each description, puzzling out the characters. There were old ploughs, giant tubs for soaking grain, washboards and many kinds of carpentry tools. All looked ancient and worn with use; handles dark and polished; metal black with age.

Some time later they emerged from the dark farmhouse, blinking in the sunshine that seemed to have grown brighter since they had been inside. The beauty of this place that belonged to neither of them was soothing, and it began to seem as though they might be able to heal what had broken.

The time was getting on towards lunchtime, and they decided to eat in a small pagoda by the lakeside. Sachiko unwrapped their picnic and laid out the food she had prepared for them. They ate companionably, but quietly, as if neither wanted to broach a subject that both were thinking about. Eventually, as Hiromichi fastidiously wiped his hands, and Sachiko cleared the empty containers from their lunch, she decided it was time.

'I went to see Harry last week, in prison.'

She wasn't sure quite how to start telling him, so she had decided to be blunt. It was only fair to be open with him. He might be angry with her, but she was still shaken by the prison visit. She couldn't quite bear to see Hiromichi's reaction, so she kept her back to him whilst she spoke.

Hiromichi was quiet for a while, and just as she had started to wonder if he'd heard her, his voice came back low and rough.

'How was that?'

'It… it was horrible. It didn't feel like it was him at all. It wasn't for very long – only about 15 minutes.'

Again the silence. She would have given anything to know what he was thinking at that moment. She turned to face him.

'Maybe I shouldn't have mentioned it. I'm sorry. I can understand that this is very upsetting for you.'

Hiromichi put his hands behind his back and examined her.

'It is a lot to take in. I have to be honest – I can't quite look at you in the same light now. You're another man's wife. Obviously, as he is alive, you didn't really have a choice about going to see him. I hope you achieved something by going there?'

Sachiko was shocked to see this new, harsher side of Hiromichi – he had always seemed so gentle.

'I was thinking about what you'd said. About the way I always run away from everything. From my parents; from my child; from Taro. My whole life. Maybe it's time for me to face up to things.'

Hiromichi's expression softened by a whisker.

'Don't get me wrong. I can't imagine what it feels like to read in the newspaper that the husband you thought was dead killed your child. Did he tell you why he did it?'

'No. He didn't seem to know himself. He didn't even seem like the same person I remember. He was mocking me. I couldn't believe we were ever together.'

Hiromichi looked back at her. He was quiet, and watchful, and she realised he was waiting for her to say more, but she wasn't sure what. She went on, halting now.

'It still doesn't make sense now. I didn't tell you… before the tsunami, I wasn't very well. I hadn't really been myself since Tashi was born. I went… away. Harry had to do everything. Oh I don't know. I can't remember. It doesn't seem like the kind of thing he could do, but he said he confessed. I feel like I never knew him at all.'

She felt hot tears well, and Hiromichi turned away, embarrassed. He gave her a few moments to compose herself, and then spoke again, his voice expressionless.

'And what will you do now?'

'What can I do? I just have to live my life, and wait for what happens next. He might hang anyway, even though they haven't found a body.'

'I see. Shall we continue then?'

Continue what? Sachiko realised he meant their tour of the gardens. He led the way and they continued their walk, but although the sun was still shining the brightness had gone out of the day. Neither of them had anything to say, and barely saw the formal cedar trees, sculpted over decades, or the ancient buildings dotted around the lake. After half an hour Hiromichi pulled up short.

'I'm not sure this is working. I think I need to think about things for a while. Shall we go back to Tokyo?'

Sachiko looked over at him. He looked sad, but contained. There was no anger in him any more. He was the same man who had held her, but a distance had grown between them.

'I'm so sorry about all of this.'

'So am I. I suppose it's not your fault. Come on – there's a train at three. We should just catch it if we hurry.'

四一

I understand now that through all of my time in Japan I have been ignoring my own lapses in good manners and mindfulness, forcing the people around me to work subtly to right things. It was just something I took for granted: from rubbish that magically moved into the correct place at 6am in the morning for collection, to shoes subtly lined up in the right direction and position to be slipped on easily. Nothing was ever spoken, but as I came to understand more Japanese I have learned that there are other ways to communicate the inconvenience of social gaffes: the sly comment; the raised eyebrow at the clumsiness of the foreigner. By playing the naïveté card, life in Japan had just magically worked for me.

I have now seen a different side, in the workings of Japanese law. There was no jury at my trial, just a judge whose decision was final. All the evidence had been marshalled and assembled into as watertight a case as possible before being presented to the court.

My interrogators were not polite. On the contrary, they went out of their way to be harsh – shouting things such as, 'Don't lie' and, 'You're getting the death penalty'. My vague answers to their questions made them visibly angry – one interrogator repeatedly slammed the table between us with his fists. It's as if they'd been told to stop at nothing to get any kind of confession – the more watertight the better – before submitting the case to the public prosecutor.

I don't know how many other prisoners are on death row; our movements are timed so that we do not encounter each other. On the rare occasions that I am allowed outside my cell the corridors are empty. The passing of time is hard to judge, with the lights always on and the enforced silence of the cell.

Strange as it may seem, I came to anticipate the interrogation sessions with something like pleasure. They break the monotony of solitary confinement. Solitary and lonely it is too, with nothing but my own thoughts for company. There have been no more visits from Tashi, and without him I cannot escape to the land of memory.

So I am forced to live only in the present, with nothing but the walls of my cell around me, and not even the distraction of a cellmate. I wish that I could trust my memory of the hours just before the tsunami. I cannot truly believe that I killed Tashi.

Dr Kitahara says I confessed to the murder during our hypnosis sessions; that I described the moment of his death many times, in different ways. I strangled him. I smashed his head against the wall. I shook him until he was blue. It was all recorded, but I have no memory of any of it. I remember looking for him before I left – the empty bouncer. My child, Tashi, had somehow vanished, to be replaced by that strange homunculus who tortured me in the wilderness. How can I remember two realities that don't agree with each other?

Gradually I learn to miss him, and Sachiko, and wonder what life would have been like if I hadn't made the decision to walk away. When Sachiko came to visit the prison she was remote, but still undeniably present. She was still beautiful, but seemed untouchable. Not the woman who lay for all those weeks with her face to the wall. Not the young student who laughed in my eyes as I learnt to Japan. How could I ever have thought I could understand her? Nothing of her feelings showed in her face, but I sensed impatience; the inconvenience of politeness. How could she be anything else with me? Lost in the gulf between our two cultures, we had nothing but love to keep us together.

四二

Sachiko's experiences of the last few months had changed her perspective on family forever, and the place that it had in her life.

Hiroko had always encouraged her to find her parents – she had been shocked that Sachiko hadn't got in touch after the tsunami, and, although she had been too polite to mention it more than once since, Sachiko knew how she felt about it. By cutting herself off from them she had shattered the family story, and broken the bonds between generations. The loss of Harry and Tashi, swept away in a single moment, had fragmented the narrative even further. She had tried to reconnect with her culture, to draw comfort from it – and logic dictated that she should close that circle by honouring her parents. It was her duty not to let the family story end like this.

And there was Hiromichi... She had a feeling it wasn't a long journey back to Hiromichi, but that there were certain compromises that both of them would have to make first; changes that were necessary before any relationship between them could work. Ten years in an increasingly unhappy marriage had taught her that. She had tried to set herself free, at any cost. Perhaps in the end the cost had been too high.

There was no denying that she was complicit in what had happened to Tashi. Weeks before the tsunami had turned their world upside down she had withdrawn from everything. How else to explain her failure to notice her husband's increasingly odd behaviour? At the time she had attributed it to the stress of the child; the insecurity of moving; not being able to write – to hatred of her. She knew now that it was she who had been in flight; her trajectory had always been away – and in order to escape she had been willing to jettison everything that made her human.

The phone rang. It was Hiromichi. She knew she should take the call, but it seemed so complicated – like a play whose lines she'd had no time to rehearse. She let it ring and ring unanswered, until she could bear its shrill admonishment no longer and fled, a coat slung carelessly about her shoulders against the March breeze.

195

四三

The hour has come. They have just informed me that today is the day of my execution. I have chosen not to have any last rites, nor to send any final letters. Tashi told me that someone would have to pay for his death, and Sachiko has been through so much already. The last thing I can do for her is make sure it's me.

The sun was shining when Sachiko received the letter – it was almost a year to the day since the tsunami. She had followed the case, of course – refused to meet with the brothers when they came over. She knew the last appeal had failed, and they always did it that way, sent a letter to the relatives after it was over. She thought maybe it was better. The American system, where prisoners made an appointment with the executioner months before, seemed so public a way to die. Sachiko recalled a rare insight into the secretive process of death row, which she had seen on television the year before. There had been the death chamber, and a small antechamber with five buttons, only one of which triggered the hatch below the feet of the condemned, so that no single prison guard would bear responsibility. In the past inmates were told about their execution several days in advance, but the practice had been stopped after a spate of suicides. Now they were informed just a few minutes before that the hour had come.

Harry would not have had much time to prepare. He would not have had a last glimpse of the sun that now slanted through her window. That room, she thought, would not have had any windows. Blank walls, and no one to witness those final moments. A quick jerk, and then just a body hanging from a rope. Had Tashi gone quickly too? With a tiny gasp she felt his passing from the world, suddenly, as if it had been yesterday and abruptly the whole crushing weight of it was upon her and the weight of all those other deaths too. It was too much to bear, but it must be borne.

The hand that held the letter clenched, became a fist that crushed the fragile sheet, heedless. And then, just as convulsively, she slapped it on the counter and made herself smooth the rumpled paper. Well, he was gone and there was an end to it.

And what of Tashi? She thought of him constantly now. Every time she saw a child she wondered what Tashi would have looked like – at six months, at one year. He would have been one now. Sachiko wasn't religious, but she realised she wanted to mark the date in some way – that it was part of coming to terms with what had happened. It seemed wrong that there was no memorial to her son's existence – not even a wooden stick with his name inscribed on it. And Harry too. How had his passage from this life been marked? He would have been executed, and cremated, but there was no mention in the letter of an *ihai*. Perhaps the condemned did not deserve to be commemorated with a spirit tablet.

There was one thing she could do to try to lay their ghosts to rest. She could bring some incense to the graveyard, and burn it for them, whilst she chanted *nembutsu* prayers first learned in childhood, when her parents would make offerings to the ancestors at New Year and *Obon*.

Jippo-o sekai nem butsu shujyo se-esshu fusha

She rehearsed the chants in her mind whilst she gathered the things she would need, and closed the door behind her, hoping that she wouldn't encounter her neighbours. It was a moment for silence, and privacy. She wasn't ready to share the contents of the letter yet, or to process the shame of being the widow of an executed prisoner, even though she knew that Mrs Takamoto wouldn't judge her for it.

Sachiko turned her steps to Aoyama Cemetery, in Minato-ku. Tall skyscrapers surrounded it, but within the cemetery were avenues of cherry trees, branches heavy with blossom reaching for the clarity of the spring sky. Now once again *sakura* was approaching. Sachiko walked on a little further, stopping to gaze above her head. A light breeze swept through, and all of a sudden petals were whirling above her head; she felt them rest like gentle benedictions on her cheeks – their touch brief but cooling.

She closed her eyes and imagined, just for a moment, that Tashi was there – running on his chubby legs along the avenue of trees; grabbing handfuls of petals, laughing, and letting them fall to the ground. The illusion was brief. Her hands knew the touch of his skin, felt again the pillow that she had used to smother his last cries.

It was the tyranny and the truth of the cherry blossoms, at last, that undid her.

And then, once again, the ground began to shake.

Acknowledgements

This book has been a long time coming – seven years in fact – and wouldn't have been possible at all without the help and encouragement of many people along the way.

Thank you to Stuart Taylor, my beloved husband, for patient listening and invaluable suggestions, and to my daughters, Ella and Matilda, for teaching me how to be a mum. Thanks to Emma Pickard for constant encouragement throughout the years, and for being a brilliant best friend.

Special thanks are due to Yukiko Tajima, for being a wonderful host in Tokyo, and a vital source of information about Japanese language and customs, as well as for reading through numerous drafts of the manuscript – I wouldn't have been able to write this book without you.

Daniel Jacobs, Scott Pack, Jakey Slater, Kit Fraser, Ivan Mulcahy, Miriam Fahey, Mike Perrett and Daniela Petracco were all early readers, and helped to validate the timeline and story; Jess Phillimore (film), Andy Dobson (music) and Bryony Morrison (script) made a beautiful trailer video to help with the crowdfunding.

This book was researched during a month-long trip to Japan that included visits to the locations covered, as well as interviews with survivors of the 2011 tsunami. I'd like to thank the people who made a foreign writer so welcome as I explored Tokyo and Tohoku in the aftermath of that event, and who helped me to understand the challenges they faced. Thanks especially to Takashi Nishida, Taka Tamayama, Graham Mckelvie and Yumi Aoyagi for their hospitality.

Thanks to the Oxford University Press for permission to reprint a quote from 'In the Forest, Under Cherries in Full Bloom' by Ango Sakaguchi, translated by Jay Rubin, published as part of *The Oxford Book of Japanese Short Stories* in 1997.

And finally, thanks to all at Unbound – especially to my brilliant and discerning editor, Annabel Wright, who has helped to keep the whole show on the road, and to Xander Cansell and Kwaku Osei-Afrifa for believing in my work and giving me a chance to bring it to a wider readership.

Patrons

Aroon Ajmera
Kurt Albrecht
Daniel Albright
Juliet Amissah
Debi Ani-Goldman
Dan Jordan Bambach
Sam Borland
Steve Bowbrick
Debbie Breen
Ian Calcutt
Chris Chalmers
Jo Clayton
Anna Cocciadiferro
Jacqueline Crooks
Will Croxford
Naila Darr
Ted Dave
Paul Bassett Davies
Rosalind Ellen Piggott Davis
Fiona Eldred
Ronnie Fairweather
James Flint
Daniela Gallenti
Joan Gibbs
Jim Gleeson
Andrew Grumbridge
Vicky Grut
Chris Heathcote
Lucy Hodge
Eric Huang
Koreen Hubbard
Manar Hussain

Johari Ismail
Daniel Jacobs
Marie James
David Kessler
Dan Kieran
Ros Lawler
Paula D Lennon
Pixie Maddison
Fran Martin
Cherie Matrix-Holt
Mike McLennan
Brendan Mcnamee
Matthew Meadows
Snorre Milde
Peter Mills
John Mitchinson
Danielle Nagler
John Neal
Hilla Neske
Ivy Ngeow
Snezana Nikolic
Godwin Nwafor
Araba Ocran
Josh On
Tatsumi Orimoto
Kwaku Osei-Afrifa
Kirkwood Paterson
Emma Pickard
Frances Pinney
Justin Pollard
Julia Roberts
Stevie Russell
Tamim Sadikali
Merlin Sinclair
Emer Stamp
Gavin Starks

Ruth Sutton
Nick Sweeney
Yukiko Tajima
Stuart Taylor
Ella & Matilda Taylor
Kevin Tillett
Nadiya Tokarska
Maria Tokarska
Sherbaan Valean
Olive Vyskocilova
Bettina Walter
Stephanie Warner
Daphne Watkins
Philip Webster
翟彧 Zhai